CRISIS IN COLOMBIA

BRYAN MARLOWE

CRISIS IN COLOMBIA

Published by Mereo

Mereo is an imprint of Memoirs Publishing

1A The Wool Market Cirencester Gloucestershire GL7 2PR
Tel: 01285 640485, Email: info@mereobooks.com
www.memoirspublishing.com, www.mereobooks.com

Crisis in Colombia

ISBN: 978-1-86151-085-3

Book jacket design Ray Lipscombe

Printed in England

I dedicate this novel to my very special American friends:
Jennie Sefton and Carl and Barbara Miller

And now the matchless deed's achieved
Determined, dared and done

Christopher Smart, English Poet (1722-71)

List of Characters in Order of their Appearance

Harry Franklin - Film Director, employed by Omega Films
Bruce Dawlish - Cameraman, employed by Omega Films
Harvey Rheingold - An actor playing leading role in Crisis in Colombia
Lionel Durrance - Film Producer for Omega Films
Jack Hardy - Chief security officer employed by Omega Films
Diego Contrero Moretta - Bandit leader and kidnapper
Rafael - Diego Contrero Moretta's lieutenant
Omar Rashid - Security officer employed by Omega Films
Hernando Gonzales - Tourist guide and bandit
Martin Walters - Harry Franklin's assistant director
Madge Burton - Lionel Durrance's personal assistant
General Alejandro Valente Zarcos - Head of the Colombian Police Force
Colonel Rolf Banderas Farrera - The general's personal staff officer
His Excellency Sir Roland Plenderleith, British Ambassador in Colombia
Peter Metcalfe - Head of Chancery in the British Embassy, Bogotá
Hugo Bickerstaff - MI6 officer in the British Embassy, Bogotá
Henri (Hank) de Poiret - CIA section leader, undercover as a hotel concierge
Sir Randolph Blandish - British Foreign Secretary
Ralph Jermayn - Senior MI6 officer working in the Foreign Office
Eli (Mac) Murphy - Former captain in the SAS
Sarah Murphy - Former captain in the Israeli Army, attached to Mossad
Manuel - A chauffeur
Marcus Parker - An alias adopted by Eli Murphy
Jorge - A helicopter pilot
Pablo - A helicopter crewman
Detective Major Carreras - A member of the Bogotá City Police Force
Detective Lieutenant Alvares - A member of the Bogotá City Police Force
Jasper Maybrick - An actor, playing a supporting role in Crisis in Colombia
Danny Bristow - Assistant cameraman, employed by Omega Films
Bartolo (Bart) - A local man working as a CIA driver
Lieutenant Barbosa - A member of the Bogotá City Police Force
Major Estrada - A member of the Bogotá City Police Force
Javier Gallado - A member of Moretta's band
Almondo Zamarco - Manager of the Fantastico Club

Peter Smurthwaite - An alias adopted by Eli Murphy

Raul - Almondo Zamarco's assistant

Alvaro - A member of Moretta's band

Aurello Bedoya - A member of Moretta's band

Gloria Duprez - An actor playing a leading role in Crisis in Colombia

Clara Purvis - A make-up artist employed by Omega Films

Carol Farley - An actor playing a supporting role in Crisis in Colombia

Ruby Benson - A continuity girl employed by Omega Films

Carlos - Hank's driver

Steve - A CIA agent

Tyler - A CIA agent

Pancho - A member of Moretta's band

Paulo - A member of Moretta's band

Paul Landers - An actor playing a supporting role in Crisis in Colombia

Barry Robbins - An actor playing a supporting role in Crisis in Colombia

Rick Morales - An actor playing a supporting role in Crisis in Colombia

Anton - A waiter in La Escudero restaurant

Miguel - A waiter at the El Cucaracha Club

Arturo Baquero - A former member of Moretta's band

Martin McFee - An alias adopted by Eli Murphy

Sabrina McFee - An alias adopted by Sarah Murphy

Sergio Almazan - Moretta's assassin

Javi - A member of Moretta's band

Captain Bejanaro - A member of the Bogotá City Police Force

Brigadier General Perez - Commander of the Bogotá City Police Force

Captain Rodrigues - A member of the Bogotá City Police Force

Carl Miller - A CIA section leader

Chuck Harden - A CIA agent

Danny Krantz - A CIA agent

Jake Feltz - A CIA agent

Earl Harper - A CIA agent

Butch Lardner - A CIA agent

Rupert Bartram - Director of MI6, SIS

Oscar Durkin - Deputy Director of the CIA

CHAPTER ONE

15 MARCH

'Cut!' shouted Harry Franklin, who was directing a film set in the Colombian jungle.

The senior cameraman, Bruce Dawlish, responded; the cameras were stilled; the cast and crew relaxed, leaned against trees or sat on the jungle floor and lit cigarettes and drank from bottles of water.

'We'll take a short break and re-shoot that scene later,' said Franklin. 'What was wrong with the scene, Harry?' Harvey Rheingold, the film's leading actor, said as he approached Franklin, a look of disbelief on his handsome face.

'If you want a straight answer, Harvey, it was a load of crap! You're supposed to be a top-bracketed actor who's paid five-million a picture. I could have got a better performance from a kid fresh out of a drama school.' Franklin lowered his voice in an attempt to avoid the members of the cast and crew hearing what he thought of the producer Lionel Durrance's much-favoured star.

'Well, what do you expect from actors who've been dumped into this stinking hell of a jungle?' Rheingold snarled.

'The rest of the cast and crew are not complaining and your leading lady is doing a great job. If the part you're

supposed to be portraying is too much for you I can…'
The rest of what Franklin said was lost in the noise of a
fusillade of gunfire. Everyone turned to see from where
it had been fired. They saw that they were surrounded by
twenty or more heavily armed men emerging from the
cover of trees and bushes. Jack Hardy, the senior security
officer with the film crew, instinctively moved to draw his
Colt automatic pistol. Several bullets struck him in the
chest before the pistol had cleared its holster. The entire
group looked on in horror as Hardy, blood spurting from
his body, fell to the ground dead.

One of the men, carrying a Kalashnikov AKSU-74
assault rifle, stepped into the clearing. 'You are all my
prisoners!' he shouted in English. 'If any of you try to run
away you will be shot!' The entire film group began
shouting and voicing their anger at what they had
witnessed. The man fired two shots in the air. The group
fell silent.

'Keep quiet!' the man shouted. Then, turning to a man
who was standing behind him, he said: 'Rafael, relieve that
young man of his sidearm and have the men collect all
those rifles leaning against trees. I suspect they are simply
film props, but the security men must have had rifles.'

Rafael summoned two of the men to collect the rifles
and ordered Omar Rashid, the young security man, to
undo his gun belt.

Omar, although lacking any experience in dealing with
such a situation, was tempted to take a chance and draw
his pistol, grab Rafael to use as a shield and try to save the

day. But the twenty rifles pointed at the film group dissuaded him – he reluctantly handed his gun belt to Rafael. 'Who is in charge of this group?' the man barked.

'I'm the director, so I suppose I am,' said Franklin, 'and if you don't release us immediately and fade away as fast as you appeared here, I'll see that the army hunt you down and charge you with murder!'

'The army!' the man laughed. 'They have been hunting for me for years, but I, Diego Contrero Moretta, govern this piece of jungle and the military are afraid to venture into this area. You say you are the director of the film? I believe it is to be called *Crisis in Colombia*, so I have been informed—so you are Harry Franklin?'

'Yes, that's me, but how do you know my name?'

Moretta laughed raucously. 'I know many things, because I have spies in every hotel and street café in Bogotá!'

'But how could you know where we would be filming today?'

'Oh, that was very easy. Hernando, your guide, is one of my most loyal followers.'

The smirking Hernando moved away from the film crew and stood beside Moretta.

'There's one thing you've forgotten, Moretta,' said Franklin. 'How do you think we got here today?'

'You came by a Chinook helicopter, which landed you in a large clearing about three hundred yards from this spot. But you won't be returning to Bogotá in it at sundown as was arranged, because the helicopter has developed engine trouble and its crewmen are all down with food poisoning. I was able to arrange for all that because, as I said, I have men wherever I might need them. Now I don't want to hear anything more from you. What I want you and your party to do is to sit down where you are and when one of my men comes around with a sack put all your belongings in it, which means cell phones, passports, wallets, watches, knives and anything that could be used as a weapon.'

'Well, you heard the man,' said Franklin. 'We've no option but to do as he says. I guess we're up shit creek in a leaking boat, without paddles.'

The filming group complied and then was told to stand and be patted all over by Moretta's men.' Now that's been done, what are you going to do with us, Moretta?'

'We are going to hold you as hostages for ransom.'

'What, stuck here in the jungle?'

'Of course not – you are going to be taken to our encampment, which is about two miles from here. Your three porters are to remain here. They have little value as hostages.'

Moretta's men assembled the filming group and Hernando took a leading position as they moved off with the bandits flanking the column and Moretta and Rafael in the rear. When they had covered about two or three hundred yards, Moretta nodded to Rafael, who returned to where they had set off.

'That was a bit of luck, boss, Moretta leaving the porters behind. They might link up with a search party,' said Franklin's assistant, Martin Walters.

Franklin nodded, but he thought differently and was not surprised to hear a volley of automatic fire a minute or so later.

'That evil bastard has had those porters killed,' Franklin whispered into Martin's ear. 'If it's the last thing I do, I'll make Moretta and his band of killers pay for what they've done today.'

CHAPTER TWO

16 MARCH

Lionel Durance, who was producing the film *Crisis in Colombia* for Omega Films, was a very worried man. He sat at his desk, in a luxurious penthouse suite in the Hilton Hotel, Bogotá, wondering why Harry Franklin, his film director, had not been in touch to tell him how the previous day's filming had gone. His personal assistant had been trying all morning to contact Franklin, but his cell phone number had been unobtainable. To make matters worse, he had been told by the airport manager that the specially chartered Chinook helicopter, which was to fly the actors and technicians back to Bogotá, had been grounded at the airport with engine trouble and its entire crew had been struck down with food poisoning and was in hospital.

His meditation was interrupted by Madge Burton, entering the room with a handful of papers. 'So what have we got in the mail today, Madge?'

'Nothing that needs your attention, sir, just the usual bunch of mail you get from writers with suggestions for film plots they want you to consider producing. But there is one letter for you, marked strictly confidential – for your personal attention. It hasn't come through the post, but was delivered by hand this morning. I haven't opened it,' she added, as she handed the grubby envelop to Durrance. He tore the envelope open, took out the single sheet of paper and read the handwritten letter aloud.

Señor Lionel Durrance,

You are advised that I hold your party of actors and film technicians as prisoners. Unfortunately, your security officer, Hardy, attempted to fire at my men and he was shot in self-defence. The three local men, working as porters for your company, ran away. The rest of your party is quite safe and if you follow my instructions will remain so. To secure their release you will need to pay me a ransom. For your leading actors it will be $5,000,000 each; $2,000,000 for each of the other actors and $1,000,000 for your director and the rest of your actors and technicians. The money is to be paid into the Bank of Panama by no later than March 31. Details of the account into which the money is to be paid will be left at the reception desk at your hotel.

For every day that payment is late one of your company will die.

Diego Contrero Moretta – March 15

Durrance dropped the letter onto his desk and ran his hands through his shock of grey hair. 'This has got to be some sort of bizarre joke, Madge. Try to raise Harry, or any of the group.'

'It's no good boss, I've tried all of their numbers and none are available. Something's gone very wrong for them and the police should be informed.'

'You're right, Madge. Ring police headquarters and get me an appointment to see the top cop.' Madge left the room, and Durrance picked up the letter and read it again. If this is true, he thought, Omega Films are in real financial trouble. If the film can't be completed, Harvey and Gloria will still have to be paid the fee they were contracted to receive, £5,000,000 each. With all the money already invested in this film, where are we going to find more to pay ransoms?

His thoughts were disturbed by the return of Madge. 'I spoke to the personal assistant, to the top man of the Colombian National Police, General Alejandro Valente Zarcos. He is not available to see you; he doesn't do interviews, but his personal staff officer, Colonel Rolf Banderas Farrera, can see you at 5.30 this afternoon.'

'Good work, Madge. It's 4.15 now and with the traffic as it is, we'd better leave now to get there in time.'

'Do you want me to go with you, boss?'

'Of course I do. I want you to take notes of anything of consequence that is said.'

They took a taxi from outside the hotel and arrived at the police headquarters at 5.20.

'We're here to see Colonel Zarcos,' Durrance said to the desk sergeant.

The sergeant glanced at a clipboard on the desk. 'Yes, sir, at 5.30,' he replied, then turned to a corporal. 'Take these people to Colonel Zarcos.'

The corporal took them to a lift and stopped it at the second floor. He led them down a short passageway to an office, tapped on the door and spoke to the woman who answered: 'Señor Durrance and his personal assistant to see Colonel Zarcos.'

The woman took them into her outer office. 'Wait here, Corporal, to take them back when their interview is over.'

She tapped on the colonel's door and a loud voice called out, 'Come in!' They entered and stood in the centre of the office. Without rising from his chair, the colonel said: 'Please be seated and tell me the nature of the matter you wish to discuss.'

Durrance and Madge sat in the two chairs positioned in front of the colonel's desk and the woman sat next to the colonel. Durrance produced the letter from Moretta and placed it on the colonel's desk.

'This will explain why we have sought an interview with the police.'

The colonel picked up the letter, read it hurriedly and sighed deeply. 'So, Moretta is up to his usual banditry. We haven't heard much lately about his activities, but it now seems from this letter that he is picking on more wealthy victims to take as hostages for ransom.'

Durrance, his eyebrows raised, said: 'Yes, Colonel, but

what are you going to do about it? He's threatened to kill my people if the ransom money is not paid before the end of this month and I'm pretty sure that Omega Films will be unable to raise the amount he demands in time!'

'Yes, it is rather an unfortunate position for you, Mister Durrance, but I'm afraid that the taking of hostages for ransom and other reasons, since the early 1970s, has been a common practice in this country and thousands of civilians, government officials and military personnel have been kidnapped. It is for this reason that our police resources do not allow us to mount major operations against the perpetrators. We see our main objectives to be in combating the drug cartels, which are responsible for many killings, of both members of the public and the police. We are also heavily engaged in preventing the smuggling of firearms into the country. And if that isn't enough, our army is engaged in a war against ten, yes ten, different left-wing guerrilla groups opposed to the government. The army does patrol the jungle areas and when they are told of what has happened to your people they will, I'm sure, do their utmost to hunt down the bandits and rescue your people. As to Moretta's threat to kill his captives, it is unlikely that he will do so. These threats are usually made by kidnappers, to intimidate their victims into paying the ransoms they want. So, I would suggest that you take steps to secure the ransom money. In the meantime I shall pass your concerns to the military authorities and, of course, keep you informed of any progress made.'

'So that's it, then? It seems to me this interview has been a complete waste of time. I shall need to take the matter up through diplomatic channels and seek advice from our ambassador.'

The colonel and his assistant rose. 'I'm sorry you feel that way, Mister Durrance, and I hope you manage to raise the money you need. I have to say I'm rather surprised that you have any doubts about doing that. From what I know about film companies, they seem to have money to burn, considering they can afford to pay actors ten million US dollars for appearing in one film.'

Durrance ignored his remark and led the way to the door. The assistant overtook him and Madge and led them to her office. 'Take them back, Corporal.'

Back at the hotel, Durrance opened his desk drawer and withdrew a bottle of 12-year-old Scotch malt whisky and two glasses. 'I don't know how you feel after that, but I need a drink. How about you, Madge, are you going to join me?'

Madge nodded and Durrance poured two generous measures.

CHAPTER THREE

17 MARCH

'His Excellency, the ambassador, will see you now Mister Durrance,' said Peter Metcalfe, the embassy's head of chancery. Metcalfe ushered Durance into the ambassador's office, invited him to be seated, then sat next to the ambassador. Another man, of early middle-age with dark hair and eyes, was in the room seated on the left of the ambassador. He eyed Durrance in a manner that seemed, to Durrance, slightly sinister.

'Good morning Mister Durrance,' said the ambassador with a half-smile. 'Peter has apprised me of the details you gave him regarding the abduction of members of your film company, who are now being held for ransom by that despicable bandit, Moretta. He seems to get away with whatever villainous act he perpetrates. I have sent a diplomatic note to the Colombian Ministry of Foreign Affairs, requesting that every effort be made to gain the early release of your people. The note has been copied to our foreign secretary, who will, no doubt, follow up on my action and take the matter to the highest level.'

'Thank you, your Excellency, I'm sure everything that can be done through diplomatic channels, will be done, but my greatest concern is that Moretta has threatened to kill the hostages if the ransom money is not paid by 31 March.'

The ambassador turned to the man on his left. 'Hugo, have you anything to add that might help to give Mister Durrance some hope for an early solution to the matter?'

'To be perfectly honest, Your Excellency, I'm afraid not. Normally, one would expect that it would not be too much of a problem for the police, supported by the military, to round up a relatively small group of bandits and deter further acts of abduction by others, who see the practice as one that provides an easy way to make money. However, both the police and the military see their first priority as the dealing with the drug cartels and the smuggling of firearms and explosives into the country from Mexico and the United States. Not only that, the Colombian Army is engaged in a war against several guerrilla and insurgent groups.'

'Thank you, Hugo. I'll leave it to you to see that everything that can be done to keep Mister Durrance informed of any progress made.' Turning to Durrance, the ambassador said: 'Be assured, Mister Durrance, Her Majesty's Government will take this matter very seriously and, I feel sure, will not rest until your people have been freed.'

'Thank you, Your Excellency,' mumbled Durrance, as he followed Metcalfe out of the office.

Returning to the hotel, Durrance saw Madge standing at the concierge's desk, engaged in conversation with him. Probably asking him about the best restaurants in Bogotá, he thought as he entered a lift to take him to the top floor. A few minutes later, Madge joined him in his office.

'You seemed to be having quite a chat with the concierge. Did he recommend any good restaurants?'

'No, I didn't ask him about restaurants. I just asked him for the present currency exchange rates. He gave them to me. Then he went on to say that he'd heard about the film group being abducted and asked if anything was being done to rescue them. He seemed to know all about that man Moretta and what's going on in this country. He was quite charming and seemed well-informed about what was happening in Colombia. His name is Henri de Poiret and he told me his home was in New Orleans. He's probably of French extraction, but proud to be an American and prefers to be called "Hank".'

'Hmm…I wonder why a seemingly well-educated and cultured American would choose to work as a concierge in a South American country, where the pay differentials for the job would be so much lower. I'd have thought there would be many hotels in New Orleans, where he could do the same job and be better paid.'

'Perhaps he's getting over a broken romance, or running away from his wife,' Madge replied with a girlish laugh. 'But on a more serious note, how did you get on at the embassy?'

'Not very well nobody seems to have any faith in the police or army doing much about rescuing our people. I'm beginning to think the best way to find them would be to hire a well-trained and experienced band of mercenaries.'

'Where could you recruit them? And if you could, surely the Colombian Government would not allow them to operate without their authority.'

'You're probably right, Madge. I have to say you do often surprise me with your logical thinking and quick appreciation of a wide range of military and other matters.'

Madge laughed. 'You never took much notice of my CV when you hired me. If you had you'd have seen that my father was a retired lieutenant colonel, who had served in the SAS. After hearing of his military history, I even thought of joining the army, but working for you is more comfortable and the pay is better.'

'What does your father do now that he's retired?'

'He's a member of the town council in Hereford, which keeps him quite busy. He also does a lot of travelling overseas. He and my mother are spending a few weeks in South Africa at present.'

'It's a pity I can't meet up with your father. He might have some ideas about how best it would be to hire some ex-SAS men to form a rescue party.'

'Yes, I'm sure you two would get on well, but I should forget about trying to recruit a private army to carry out unauthorized operations in a foreign country.'

'Yes, I suppose you're right, Madge. You usually are. We'll just have to wait and see what tomorrow brings.'

CHAPTER FOUR

18 MARCH

Donald Forster, the British Foreign Secretary's chief of staff, tapped discreetly on Sir Randolph Blandish's door. 'Come in!' boomed Blandish's voice from within.

Forster entered carrying a sheaf of papers. 'What have you got for me this morning, Donald?'

'It's mostly routine bumf, sir. But there is a follow-up from our ambassador in Bogotá, on the report we received regarding film company employees, who were abducted by bandits in the Colombian jungle three days ago and are now being held for ransom. The ambassador forwards a *cri de coeur* from the film's producer, Lionel Durrance.'

Blandish sighed deeply. 'Why on earth was the man making a film in a country that's undergoing all manner of serious problems in dealing with drug cartels, gun-running and cases of hundreds of government employees and tourists being abducted?'

'Yes, sir, I agree, he was asking for trouble filming where he was. There's only one thing he got right and that's the title of his film.'

'Well, what's it called, Donald?'

'Most aptly, sir, *Crisis in Colombia*,' Donald answered with a wide grin.

Blandish gave a short laugh. 'So what's the gist of Durrance's letter?'

'He's pleading poverty. He says his company, Omega Films, is unlikely to be able to raise the ransom demanded. Apparently the company has invested most of its working capital in the film and has foolishly agreed to pay its top two stars five million pounds each, even if the film is not made. And the way things are going it looks as though it won't be made!'

'What is the total ransom demanded?'

'We have a list of the people being held and the individual amounts the bandit leader has stipulated for each person and the total figure amounts to thirty-million pounds!'

Blandish 'phewed' loudly. 'In the present economic climate there's no way the PM would authorize that amount to be paid to a bloody bandit,' he said. 'What other options have we?'

'We could send a stronger note to the Colombian government and hope they would ginger up their military and police forces to make greater efforts to locate the hostages and deal with those holding them.'

'Yes, do that, Donald, but I doubt it will motivate them to greater efforts.'

'We could try to negotiate with the bandits, but making contact with them would be extremely difficult. They'll not want to come out in the open until the ransom money is ready for them to collect.'

'Yes, I'm sure you're right there.'

'I suppose that using a unit of our special forces to mount a rescue operation is out of the question, sir?'

'Yes, completely out of the question. I doubt the Colombians would want to lose face. And if they did agree, our men wouldn't have a clue as to where to start searching. Not only that, the presence of foreign troops operating in the jungle would probably soon be found out by the bandits. But your suggestion does give me an idea. Get on to MI6 and request that Hugo Bickerstaff or Ralph Jermayn report to me ASAP!'

Forster left the office to make the call. Later that afternoon, Forster ushered Ralph Jermayn into Blandish's office and said, 'Ralph Jermayn of MI6, sir.'

'Thank you, Donald. You may leave us now and get some tea and biscuits sent up.'

Forster walked out of the office with a sulky look, thinking, what is the boss up to now that he doesn't want to share with me?

'Take a seat, Ralph, and tell me what you're doing these days?'

'Oh, much the same as I've always done, sir, but since I was promoted to a section head in the department, I've been office bound in the ministry most of the time.'

'Well, that's the way it goes old chum, as you move up the ladder. Tell me, do you have any contact with that colleague of yours, Hugo what's-his-name?'

'You must mean Hugo Bickerstaff, sir.'

'Yes, that's the chap. What's he up to these days?'

'He's on very active service, operating as a "friend" in the embassy in Bogotá.'

'Really? That's interesting.'

'I don't want to be disrespectful, sir, but I have a lot to do this afternoon, so I'd be most grateful if you would come to the point of why you wanted to see me, or Hugo?'

Blandish's face reddened slightly. 'Oh, I am sorry, but what I have to discuss with you is most important and, of course, highly confidential, so I suggest you ring your office and tell them you won't be available this afternoon. When you've done that I'll put you in the picture.'

Jermayn made the call, then sat back in his chair and looked enquiringly at Blandish.

'Firstly, do you have any sort of contact with that ex-SAS captain, Eli Mac Murray, or is it Murphy?'

'Not really, sir. He and his wife have invited me to their home in Cambridge a couple of times.'

'What's he doing now?'

'Not a lot. He still gives the occasional lecture at the university. And he and his wife spend time abroad.'

'What shape is he in? Would you say he'd be up to undertaking another covert operation?'

'Well, he still has a bit of trouble with his gammy left leg, which was severely injured when he and his family were victims of a terrorist bomb in Casablanca a few years ago, but in spite of that, for a man in his mid-forties he's in better shape than most men half his age. But what have you got in mind for him, sir?'

'You will, of course, have heard all about the group of film actors and technicians, who were filming in Colombia, being abducted and held for ransom.'

'Yes, I've seen the report from our embassy in Bogotá.'

'Well, you can see that something must be done to rescue these British Nationals, before the kidnappers start killing them if the ransom is not paid by 31 March.'

'Yes, sir, I understand the position, but had thought that Omega Films, the company these people are working for, would pay the ransoms.'

'I'm afraid there's little chance of that happening; the company is in a poor financial state because they have invested heavily in this production, hoping that if it is successful it will give them a good return on their investment.'

'Well, if the Colombian Army and police can't manage to deal with the kidnappers, how can one man, tough, battle-hardened and resourceful as he is, be expected to rescue the group?'

'Don't be so negative, Ralph. Aren't you forgetting how he managed to rescue that British newspaperman and his wife, who were being held prisoner by the Syrian Secret Service?'

'No, sir, I remember all the details of that successful operation, but I also remember that he managed to get the support of the Syrian rebel forces to carry out the rescue.'

'Yes, Ralph, but that support was reciprocal. He successfully led units of the rebel forces against the government forces.'

'That is so, but I don't think he'd get the same support from the Colombian authorities.'

'Perhaps not, but we've nothing to lose. We simply

persuade him to take on the job, but without overt support from us. If he's successful we can claim some of the credit, which will earn us a lot of votes in the next election.'

'So, what do you want me to do, sir?'

'Go and see him without delay and provide him with the latest information on the situation pertaining in Colombia. Your man, Hugo, in Bogotá, can update you and provide covert support to Murphy. But whatever happens, this operation must be kept in-house, and by that I mean not known to anyone outside MI6 and me. Do you understand, Ralph?'

Jermayn sighed silently. 'Yes, sir, perfectly, but there's just one thing we haven't mentioned, and that's what about Murphy's wife?'

Blandish closed his eyes in thought before he replied. 'Well, from what I've heard about her, when she's working with her husband she cuts the odds against their success by half. But don't mention anything about her to Murphy. That'll be their decision to decide whether or not she'll take part in the rescue operation. Now off you go!' Jermayn rose from his chair and without a word walked out of the office.

CHAPTER FIVE

19 MARCH

Mac and Sarah were watching a news report about the abduction of the Omega Film Company's group of actors and technicians in Colombia. The doorbell rang.

'We're not expecting any callers, are we, Sarah?'

Sarah shook her head. 'I'll go,' she said, as she hurried to the front door.

She returned a minute later, followed by Ralph Jermayn. 'We've got a surprise visitor, Mac.'

'Yes, forgive me for not getting in touch with you before I left,' said Jermayn.

'That's okay, Ralph, you're always welcome. We look forward to your rare visits. It gives us an opportunity to hear from you what's really going on in the world of intrigue and mayhem,' said Mac, as he silenced the television. 'Take a seat, Ralph, and tell us what brings you to our remote abode?'

'I see from what you've been viewing that you are following that case of the film company being held for ransom in Colombia, Mac.'

'Yes, it's a nasty mess for someone to put right. The producer must be bonkers filming in the Colombian jungle. Apart from the resident wild life, the place is crawling with the worst of the Colombian underworld, high on drugs and armed to the teeth with smuggled weapons. I'm not surprised that the Colombian Army is uneasy about venturing too far into unknown and dangerous territory.'

'Well, you should know all about that, Mac. You've spent more than half your life doing just that.'

'Yes, and there are times when I'd like to be doing that again. I'm finding this unexciting and tame existence rather boring.'

'You mean you'd be prepared to carry out a similar rescue operation to the one you did in Syria?'

'Yes, why not? That's if Sarah agrees and…' Mac stopped speaking as Sarah entered the room with a trolley laden with drinks and snacks.

'Seeing Sarah bringing in the refreshments reminds me to ask you how Safwana, the young woman you brought back from Syria to work as your maid, is settling in to your way of life.'

'She's a real treasure, Ralph. We're really lucky to have her. She's out doing one of her favourite chores   the weekly shopping at the local supermarket. Now, to get back to what you two were plotting while I was in the kitchen. Now, to what am I to agree?'

'Oh, Ralph was just talking about the kidnapping of that party of film-makers in Colombia. He thought we might be interested in mounting an operation to rescue them.'

'Surely that should be a Colombian Army and police force's job!'

'Yes, of course it should be, but they make the excuse that they have too many other commitments, which must take priority over rescuing people stupid enough to have got themselves kidnapped. They think that the film company should pay the ransom.'

'And why shouldn't they? They make enough money to be able to pay their top stars millions for making a film.'

'I know, but this company, Omega Films, has sunk most of its capital into making this particular film and is unlikely to be able to raise the money to pay the amount the kidnappers have demanded. And, as you saw on the television news, they are threatening to kill a hostage for every day past the deadline, 31 March, for paying the ransom.'

'Am I to take it that apart from sending diplomatic notes to the Colombian government, our government is not willing to intervene in this matter in any way?'

'You've got it in one, Mac; they've sent me to try to persuade you to attempt a rescue of the hostages.'

Mac turned to Sarah. 'Has Ralph persuaded us?'

'I know he's persuaded *you*, but before you jump in with both feet, we need to know a lot more about what we'd be facing. Neither of us has ever been to South America. We don't speak Spanish and we don't know what sort of opposition we'd be up against. And, more importantly, what support, if any, would we get from MI6 agents working in Colombia?'

'Well, Sarah has spoken for us both, Ralph. So what can you tell us that will give us any chance of carrying out a successful rescue mission?'

'You'd be supplied with detailed maps of the region in which it is believed the hostages are being held. It is known that the leader of the kidnappers can speak and write English, as do most of the government officials, and the senior military and police officers, with whom you might need to liaise. Although, I have to say, you are not likely to get much help from them. You will, however, get covert support from our agents in the field and Omega Films will provide the funding for the operation. As to the opposition, the leader of the kidnappers is a well-known criminal, who has about fifty fighting men under his command. Some of these men are believed to have infiltrated the army and police forces and he also has a network of spies working in hotels and restaurants.'

'What British agents are stationed there?'

'Hugo Bickerstaff, whom you've met, is in charge of a small section of "friends" in the embassy.'

'Yes, I remember him. But if he is only authorized to carry out covert support he's not likely to be much help if we find we're engaged in active operations.'

'He'll do his best, Mac, and he's no slouch when he's in action. But you have to remember that whatever happens, Her Majesty's Government will claim that they have no knowledge of your mission.'

'Are the CIA very active there?'

'They certainly are – in more ways than one,' Jermayn laughed. 'They're assisting the authorities in trying to deal with the drug cartels and cut off the supply of arms which are being smuggled into the country from Mexico and Florida.'

'That doesn't sound like anything to laugh about, Ralph.'

'No, it wasn't for the lot who were there covering their president's visit to Colombia. They were found to have engaged prostitutes to share their hotel rooms. As a result they were sent back to the U.S. and sacked for misconduct!'

'When you think of all the other naughty things the CIA get up to, that seems a bit over the top! But your mention of smuggled arms prompts me to ask, how will I be able to get what I'll need?'

'No real problem there, Mac. We'll probably be able to arrange for small arms to be brought into the country in the diplomatic bag. Anyway, the country is awash with all manner of weapons and explosives, so I'm sure you'll get your hands on what you need from one source or another. Oh, there's just one other thing I should mention.'

'And what's that, Ralph?'

'You might not be aware, because you've not operated in this continent before, but the Colombian Army is battling ten different guerrilla and insurgent groups. Most of which are not sloppy untrained forces. The FARC forces are wealthy, well-equipped and highly trained.'

'I do read the quality newspapers and *Time Magazine*, so I have heard all about them. Could I expect any support from them?'

'That would be very unlikely, so I should steer clear of them if you can.'

'Hells Bells, Ralph, your briefing is not doing my

confidence any favours! Can you tell me one thing that might give me something to work on?'

'Yes, come to think of it, there is, Mac. The film-makers were flown by helicopter to a jungle area north-east of Bogotá. The area was recommended to them by a guide, named Hernando Gonzales. He touts for business in hotel lobbies to guide tourists in the jungle areas. I rate him as a shifty bugger and wouldn't be surprised if he'd deliberately led the film company into an ambush.'

'It was reported on television that the Chinook helicopter was grounded at the airport and couldn't be used to bring the company back after they had finished filming for the day. So, to my mind, Ralph, that means Hernando must still be with the kidnapped group.'

'I shouldn't be too sure about that, because the rebels and others have access to small helicopters and Moretta could have sent Hernando back to the city, probably to the Hilton, where Lionel Durrance is staying.'

'Well, it sounds like it's going to be one hell of a job for someone!'

'Yes, and it's all yours if you want it. But I'm afraid I need an answer before I return to the ministry, because the time is fast running out for those film-makers.' Mac looked at Sarah. 'Shall we give it a try?'

'Yes, because if we don't I'll never hear the last of it.'

'Great!' Jermayn said. 'I've already booked you first class on British Airways' mid-morning flight from Heathrow to Bogotá and a luxury suite, next to Lionel Durrance's at the Hilton, has been booked for you.'

'Why Ralph, you've been very artful, taking us for granted!' Sarah said with a laugh.

'I'm sorry, Sarah, but being artful is a very necessary skill for MI6 agents.'

'Do we need visas for this trip, Ralph?' Mac cut in.

'Yes, and they are being held for you at the First Class desk at Heathrow.'

'What about currency?'

Jermayn withdrew an envelope from his inside pocket and handed it to Mac. 'There's five grand in sterling here to meet your immediate expenses and Durrance will give you all the Pesos you may need in Colombia. And he has said that he'll give you a seven-figure bonus if you successfully pull off the rescue.'

Mac gave a low whistle. 'That's a lot of money, but if Omega Films are in the hands of an administrator when we get back, we might have to settle for a lot less.'

'Don't worry about that! If you do pull it off, you'll have earned it and Durrance will foot the bill. Now, I'd better leave you to get your packing done. You won't need to take too much with you, because you can buy all the appropriate clothing you'll need in Bogotá.'

Jermayn took his cell phone out of his jacket pocket and quickly tapped a number. 'All is well, sir, they are leaving tomorrow morning.' Replacing his phone he said: 'I was just keeping the Foreign Secretary informed. He will instruct our ambassador in Bogotá to have you met at the airport. It's now just for me to wish you bon voyage and good luck on your mission.' Mac and Jermayn shook hands and Jermayn gave Sarah a hug and kissed her on the cheek.

CHAPTER SIX

20 MARCH

Mac and Sarah quickly passed the security, customs and immigration checks and walked towards the exit of the airport. They stopped as a man wearing a chauffeur's uniform raised a cardboard notice at eye level. Written on it was the name – "Murphy". 'That's us,' said Mac.

The man smiled and lowered the board. 'My name is Manuel and I am to take you to the Hilton Hotel,' he said, turning towards the exit door and leading them onto the street, where a black Rolls Royce was parked. Manuel took their baggage. 'You're travelling light,' he said with a smile as he stowed it into the car's roomy boot.

'Yes, by travelling light we find it gets us out of the airport quicker,' replied Mac for something to say.

Arriving at the hotel, Manuel led them to a man who was talking to the concierge. Mac immediately recognized him as Hugo Bickerstaff.

'Welcome to Colombia, Mac, Sarah,' he said with a smile. Moving away from the concierge's desk he said, 'When you've checked in I'll join you in your suite and update you on recent developments. After that I'll introduce you to Lionel Durrance; he's in the suite next to yours.'

'We'd like a few minutes to unpack and get freshened up before we meet anyone else,' said Sarah.

'Yes, of course, I'll let you get booked in and then wait in the cocktail lounge while you do what you have to do. Manuel has got your suite number and has arranged for your baggage, such as it is, to be taken there as soon as you've collected your keys.'

'That's fine, Hugo, join us in our suite in about 20 minutes,' said Mac. He and Sarah went to the reception desk and Hugo returned to the concierge's desk.

'This is all very pleasant,' said Sarah, surveying the suite.

'Yes, and it's very convenient being next door to Durrance,' Mac replied. 'You have your shower and change your clothes while I unpack.'

'Aren't you having a shower?' Sarah exclaimed.

'Yes, if there's room in the shower stall for two,' Mac grinned.

'You've always managed before, whatever the size,' said Sarah, as she hurriedly stripped and went to the bathroom.

Mac followed suit and they spent five minutes splashing about in the shower like two virginal newlyweds discovering sex for the first time.

They had barely got dressed before there was a tap on their door. 'That's Hugo,' said Mac, admitting him to the room.

'I'm supposed to brief you on the present developments regarding the kidnappings. But the fact is, there haven't been any.' Bickerstaff slumped into an armchair.

'You mean the army and the police haven't come up with anything!'

Bickerstaff nodded. 'That's right absolutely nothing!'

'Then we'd better have words with Durrance!' Mac snapped.

They left the suite and Bickerstaff tapped on the door of the neighbouring suite. Madge opened the door. 'Please come in. Mister Durrance is anxious to get you started on your mission to rescue our people.'

Durrance got up from his desk and met them in the centre of the room. 'So you're the intrepid duo I've heard so much about,' he smiled as he extended his hand. Mac and Sarah shook his hand. 'Please be seated and I'll fill you in with all the information I have.'

'I don't think that will be necessary, Mister Durrance. I was fully briefed by Ralph Jermayn of MI6 before we left the UK and Hugo has told me there is nothing new to report. But I have several questions I'd like to ask you.'

'Then please fire away, Mister Murphy.'

'Let's not waste time being overly polite. My name is Mac, my wife's name is Sarah, okay, Lionel?'

'Yes, of course! Please feel free to address me thus.'

'The first thing I want from you, Lionel, is a full list of the abductees. Their job title, physical description, age, and any personal weaknesses or hang-ups they may have, which might aggravate their situation.'

'I anticipated that request and Madge has already produced a comprehensive dossier on each of our people.'

Madge took a large envelope from a tray on Durrance's desk and handed it to Mac. 'Everything you need is here, Mac.'

'Thank you, Madge.'

'May I offer you refreshment?' asked Durrance.

'Colombian coffee is supposed to be very good, so perhaps we should try that,' Sarah said. Hugo and Mac nodded.

'Madge, get room service to send up coffee and biscuits for five,' Durrance said.

'Can we get on with what I'm here for?' said Mac with an edge of impatience in his voice.

'Yes, of course, please do, Mac.'

'Who chartered the helicopter and hired the guide?'

Durrance looked slightly taken aback by the question. 'Well, I rang the airport manager with our requirement for the largest helicopter available and he came up with the offer of the Chinook. The guide, Hernando Gonzales, offered his services when he heard we were planning to film in the jungle.'

'Were any police checks made about Gonzales?'

'No, it wasn't considered necessary. He was always hanging about in reception and the hotel staff said that he frequently took tourists out and there had been no complaints about his service.'

'Have you any idea of his home address?'

'No, but Madge might have it.'

'No, I don't know,' said Madge.

'Then how was he to be paid?'

'Harry Franklin, the director, was to do that and also pay for the hire of the helicopter.'

'Now I've heard that Omega Films is unlikely to be

able to pay the ransoms demanded. Is that entirely true?'

'No doubt about that at all. The company has invested too much in the film and in the financial circumstances prevailing in the UK and the USA, they are not likely to be able to raise a loan sufficient enough to meet the ransom.'

'So, unless the army or police can rescue your people before 31 March, they are to die, one by one, at the hands of this man Moretta and his gang?'

'Yes, Mac; that is the position and now it's my turn to ask the questions. What are you going to do about rescuing them?'

'Be assured, Lionel, Sarah and I will do everything possible to find and free them, but it is not my practice to discuss my detailed plans with anyone unless they are actively engaged in the operation with us.'

'Find them, please find them! If you do, Omega films have promised to pay you one million pounds.'

Mac looked at his watch. 'Well, it's time for dinner and when we've had that we'll be turning in for the night. We need a good night's sleep, for I fancy we'll have a very busy day tomorrow.'

CHAPTER SEVEN

21 MARCH

'So, what's the plan for today, Mac?' said Sarah as she dried her near black tresses.

'We need some clothes suitable for jungle trekking. So, I suggest you check with reception the best place to get what we need. Don't forget to get the bush jackets at least a size larger. We'll need that extra space to carry weapons. Get three sets of what we need and some strong waterproof boots. Oh yes, and a first-aid pack that we can carry.'

'I'll need some money in local currency.'

'Yes, I'll give you a couple of thousand in sterling to change at reception. When I see Durrance later I'll get a good supply of Pesos. We may need some for bribes and sweeteners.'

'What are you going to be doing while I'm shopping?'

'I shall be out combing the city, trying to locate Hernando's hideaway,' said Mac with a wide grin.

'That sounds like it might be one of your "in" jokes, Mac.'

'Yes, but I have to admit it's not one of my better ones.'

Sarah finished tidying her hair and dressing and made ready to leave the suite. 'I'm off then, Mac.'

'Okay, I'll try to get back at lunch time, but if I'm not back get your lunch in the restaurant and wait for me up here. You can follow the television news and see if there's any more information about the abductees.'

After Sarah left, Mac rang reception for an English newspaper, which proved to contain nothing new about the kidnapping.

He rang the embassy and asked to speak to Bickerstaff. He was put through and a woman answered the phone. 'Who's calling, please?'

'My name is Murphy and I'd like to speak to Hugo.'

'What is the nature of your business, Mister Murphy?'

'Hugo knows, so please put him on!' Mac snapped back.

A minute passed and Hugo came on the line. 'Mac, I hope you're not going to make this a regular habit. Only ring if you have a genuine emergency to deal with!'

'This *is* an emergency! So get off your bureaucratic high horse and listen!'

'Okay, Mac   make it snappy! Walls have ears, especially in embassies.'

'I need some handguns and some spare ammo and I can't wait for your diplomatic bag.'

There was a distinct pause before Hugo replied. 'What have you in mind?'

'The best you can get your hands on. You must have an arsenal of sorts in the embassy. If you've got one, I'd favour a Glock, either 17 or 18.'

'No, we've not been equipped with those yet. I could

let you borrow my own Smith and Wesson Mk 22, Model 0 "Hush Puppy". It's the US Navy Seals' favoured weapon. As you might guess from its name, it can be fitted with a sound moderator and has an eight round detachable box magazine. I also have a shoulder holster for it.'

'That'll do fine. But I'll need more than one magazine.'

'I have only three and a box of 50 rounds.'

'Can you get them to me this morning?'

'Yes, I'll bring them to you in about twenty minutes. I wouldn't trust anyone else with my personal weapon. I bought the pistol and ammo from a Navy Seal officer who had used it with deadly effect in silencing sentries in Vietnam.'

'That's just what I need, an experienced gun.'

While waiting for Hugo, Mac spent time poring over a street map of Bogotá.

True to his word, Hugo arrived after about twenty minutes carrying a leather briefcase.

Mac took the pistol out, worked the action, fitted the sound moderator and a magazine, then applied the safety catch. 'Have you ever used it, Hugo?'

'No, I've never had the need to shoot anyone, but I wouldn't want to lose it.'

'Anyway, thanks for the loan of it. I promise to take care of it.'

After Hugo had left, Mac put on the shoulder holster, disconnected the sound moderator and practised drawing the pistol.

Time for me to start looking for Hernando, he thought,

and went down to the reception desk. 'Have you any idea of the address of Hernando Gonzales, the guide?' he asked a young woman receptionist.

The woman looked puzzled. 'No, I'm sorry, I don't know. I should ask the concierge. He seems to know everyone who comes into the hotel.'

Mac thanked her and went to the concierge's desk. He was reading a book and when Mac stopped in front of the desk he put the book in the desk drawer and stood up. 'Good morning Mister Murphy, and what can I do for you?'

'I've been here for less than 24 hours, I've never spoken to you, and yet you know my name; how come?'

'I make it my business to know all our guests. Now what can I do for you?'

'What is your name?'

'Henri de Poiret, but I prefer to be called "Hank".'

'Right, Hank, have you any idea where a guide named Hernando Gonzales lives? I've been told he hangs about in here touting for business.'

'Where do you want to be guided? There are many guides in the city and most specialise on one particular area. Hernando usually takes tourists into the jungle.'

'Okay, that's where I want to go, so where does he live?'

'Come with me to my office. I have a large scale city map there and can show you exactly where to find him.' He unlocked the door behind his desk and led Mac into a small sparsely furnished office with a desk, two chairs, a small bookcase and a wall-mounted map of Bogotá and the surrounding countryside. Hank switched on the lamp above the map and pointed to a street with a pencil. 'He lives in the small block of flats at the end of Calle Fontano.'

'Have you any idea of the number of his flat?'

'No, but most flats have the name of the occupant below the door number.'

'Well, thank you for your trouble, Hank.'

'Just a minute, Mister Murphy, a little advice take great care when you are with this man in the jungle.'

'Why, what do you know about him?'

'I know that he works for a bandit, named Diego Moretta and that you have been commissioned by Omega Films to search for a group of film-makers who have been kidnapped and are now being held somewhere in the jungle. It's my guess that this man was responsible for leading the group into an ambush.'

'Well. I'll be damned. You knowing what you do must make you an under-cover CIA agent.'

'Yes, and I want to stay that way. I've given you this advice because I know all about you and have worked with Hugo.'

'Well, isn't it a small world! It's my guess you're not here to help rescue kidnapped tourists, whatever their nationality, but you're trying to drive the drug cartels out of business and stop the flow of firearms being smuggled here from the USA.'

'Yes, that's right, and we are also trying to stop

communist guerrillas from overthrowing Colombia's right-wing government.'

'That could be a tall order and I'd have thought that after Korea, Cuba, Vietnam, El Salvador and similar left-wing states, you would by now have given up trying to change the world to how you think it should be.'

'I'm not like you Murphy, a free agent; I'm a government employee, who does what his commander-in-chief orders. However, there's no reason for us not to exchange information. We do it all the time with your MI5 and MI6.'

'Okay, Hank, I owe you one for the information you've just passed to me, so if I run into any drug barons or gun-runners I'll give you the tip-off. And you've no need to worry about me breaking your cover. I'm ex-SAS and was trained to keep mum. By the way, you may call me Mac and I'll say au revoir, because I'm sure we'll meet again, Hank.'

Mac walked out of the office and Hank followed him after locking the door.

'Goodbye Mister Murphy, I do hope you enjoy your trek in the jungle.'

Mac got into a taxi that was queuing outside the hotel and told the driver to take him to Calle Fontano. He stopped the driver a few yards from the block of flats that Hank had mentioned, paid the driver and walked into the block. He noted that the doors of each apartment were numbered and below the number was the name of the occupant. He was on the third floor before he found the door with Hernando Gonzales' name on it. He pressed the doorbell and a few seconds later a short, slightly built, swarthy faced and black haired man of about forty opened the door.

'Señor Gonzales?' Mac asked with a smile.

The man looked hard at Mac before he replied. 'Yes, that is I, and who are you?'

Mac smiled again. 'My name is Marcus Parker and I have been advised that you offer your services as a guide and can be engaged to take tourists into the jungle.'

Gonzales seemed to relax. 'So, you wish to hire my services?'

'Yes, please. I should explain that my wife and I are very interested in the country's wild life and want to take photographs of animals in their natural habitat.'

'That can be arranged. You'd better come in and we can discuss terms for my hire.'

He led the way into an untidy sitting room with a smell of fish and body odour permeating the air.

'Take a seat, Mister Parker, and tell me when you wish to go on your tour. I should mention that the jungle areas are some distance from Bogotá and it is usual to go by helicopter, land in a jungle clearing and then proceed on foot for as far as you wish to go. Of course, the hire of a helicopter and crew is very expensive.'

'The cost is of no consequence to me. I'm prepared to pay whatever it costs to get photographs of leopards and other feline creatures.'

Gonzales licked his lips. 'That being the case, I'm sure

we can come to a mutually satisfactory arrangement, Mister Parker.'

'How soon can we make the trip?'

'As soon as you wish; I have good contacts at the airport and never have difficulty in hiring a helicopter.'

'Then please arrange for a take-off time of 10.00 hours tomorrow morning.'

'I'll see to that straight away. Of course, I shall require a deposit to make the booking.'

'How much do you want?'

'Two-hundred and seventy-five thousand Pesos is the normal amount required.'

Mac gave a low whistle. 'How much is that in Sterling?'

'One hundred pounds, but you may pay in any currency, US Dollars, Euros.'

'I'll pay you in Sterling,' Mac said as he reached into his jacket pocket for his wallet. He withdrew two fifty-pound notes and handed them to Gonzales.

Gonzales snatched the money from Mac's hand and stuffed it into his hip pocket. 'Until tomorrow then, Mister Parker,' said Gonzales as he turned to lead Mac to the front door.

'Hang on old chap, there's one or two questions I have for you. How many crewmen does the helicopter have?'

'Um, er, just two, a pilot and a flight engineer.'

'Are they armed?'

'I don't know for sure, but they are quite likely to have handguns on the plane. They won't be accompanying us on the jungle trek, but will remain with their aircraft. If you are worrying about your safety, I shall be armed with an automatic rifle.'

'Do you mean an assault weapon? That seems a lot of firepower for possibly having to shoot a wild cat that doesn't want its photo taken,' Mac said with a brief grin.

'Perhaps so, but there have been rare cases when tourist parties have been attacked by bandits. But I assure you and your wife will be in safe hands with me as your guide and guard.'

'Okay, then, we'll be at the private airport at 0945 hours tomorrow morning.'

'There's just one thing you ought to know; you need to be appropriately dressed for the jungle,'

'Yes, I know, my wife is out buying what we need this morning. She's also buying packed lunches and water.'

'Well, you seem to be well organised, Mister Parker. I'll meet you at the reception desk at the private airport at 9.45. The helicopter crew will have already submitted their flight plan, so there will be no delay in us taking off at ten o'clock.'

Gonzales opened the door, they exchanged goodbyes and Mac went down to the street to hail a taxi.

When Mac arrived back at the hotel he found Sarah, laden with large shopping bags, getting out of a taxi. A porter dashed out from the hotel with a trolley and loaded the bags. Mac joined Sarah and told the man the number of their suite.

Back in their suite Sarah unpacked all the clothing and

laid it out on the bed. 'I tried mine in the shop, but you'd better see that everything, particularly the boots, fit you.'

Mac quickly changed into the clothes and put on the boots. 'Yes, everything fits a treat. And I see that you got extra chest sizes to allow space for weapons we'll be carrying.'

'I haven't got a weapon!' Sarah said. 'I'll look as though I've slimmed out of my clothes.'

'You can always stick the packed lunches behind your bush jacket,' Mac laughed.

'Trust you to make a joke out of it!'

'Okay, it's serious stuff from now on. What we need is a camera that you can hang from your neck. Remember, you're supposed to be taking photos of wild life. I noticed there is an expensive gift shop on the first floor. You should be able to get a suitable digital camera there. You never know, we might see something or somebody we want a picture of.'

'What about some lunch? I've not even had a coffee all morning.'

'Neither have I! I'll meet you in the dining room after you've bought your camera.'

It was mid-afternoon before Mac and Sarah finished their lunch.

'I don't think we should do much this afternoon. After you've practised using your new camera and we've got all our jungle clothing ready to put on in the morning, I think we should take a nap and if you feel up to it later, we could watch a late film.'

'Yes, that sounds about all I want to do for the rest of today. You haven't told me what you're planning to do tomorrow. I just hope you don't intend to take any unnecessary risks. After all, you've no idea how much you can trust that guide. If he did lead those film people into a trap, he might be planning to do something like that with us.'

Mac put his arms around Sarah. 'Don't worry, darling, I think I've got the measure of him. He's just greedy for money and he thinks I'm a rather simple-minded tourist who's got more money than street wisdom. I might have to prove him wrong about that, but I'll make sure I'm ready for anything he may have in mind.'

CHAPTER EIGHT

22 MARCH

Mac and Sarah were up, showered, and dressed in their new clothing and eating breakfast before 8 o'clock.

Passing the reception, they noticed that Hank, the concierge, was at his desk. When he saw them he joined them as they stood waiting for the lift.

'My, my, you two do look like jungle trekkers. What are you looking for today?' he asked, giving Mac a sly wink.

'We'll be looking for wild life, to photograph. Sarah wants to make good use of her new camera,' Mac replied,

'Well, I do hope you have some success. But be very careful; the jungle is full of all manner of wild life and some of it is very dangerous.'

The lift arrived before Mac could think of a reply and just waved as they stepped into the lift.

Back in their suite, Mac rang Durrance. Madge answered: 'You're up early; my master hasn't risen yet. What are your plans for today?'

'We're flying into the jungle with that guide. I'm hoping I might learn something about where the kidnappers might have taken the hostages.'

'I'll let Lionel know as soon as he gets up. He plans to spend the day ringing every film producer he knows to get donations or loans from them. Take care in the jungle. We'll look forward to your news when you return.'

'We'll be in touch and see you later, Madge.'

Back in their suite, Sarah stuffed their lunch boxes and first-aid kit into a backpack. Mac put on his shoulder holster; put the sound moderator in his hip pocket and two spare ammo clips in his trousers pockets. He checked the action on his pistol, slid a round into the breach and applied the safety catch.

'Are you ready to go, Sarah?' Mac said, looking at his watch.

'If you are, Mac.'

'Then let's go!'

They got into a waiting taxi and Mac told the driver to take them to the private airfield.

The journey took about thirty minutes and the driver stopped opposite the reception area.

They entered the building and saw Gonzales talking to one of the female receptionists. He was carrying a large canvas bag strapped to his left shoulder. His weapon, thought Mac. Gonzales turned and saw them. 'Good morning, Mister Parker and I'm very pleased to meet you, Señora Parker.'

Sarah replied with a smile.

As they crossed the pan to where the helicopter was standing, Mac identified it as a Eurocopter Lakota helicopter and whispered to Sarah, 'It seats nine so it should be a comfortable flight.'

Turning to Gonzales, Mac asked, 'Is everything ready for take-off?'

'Yes, the crew have filed their flight plan, refuelled the aircraft and the air traffic controller has cleared them to take-off in fifteen minutes.'

As they approached the aircraft, the crew came to meet them. Gonzales introduced them to the crew. The pilot, Jorge, was late middle-aged with a heavily lined face partially covered by a grizzled beard and a crop of thick greying hair. The flight engineer, Pablo, was about thirty-five, slightly built, dark skinned, and with a crop of black curly hair.

'We're ready to take off, so please climb aboard,' said Jorge.

Jorge waited until everyone was seated before he joined them. Pablo sat next to him; Gonzales, on his own, behind them and Mac and Sarah behind him.

The helicopter took off with a roar of the engine and a loud threshing noise of the rotor blades. Jorge took the aircraft up to about five-thousand feet and set the speed to about 130 knots.

'What is its range on a tankful of fuel, Jorge?' Mac asked.

'Oh, er, up to about three-hundred and seventy nautical miles,' answered Jorge over his shoulder.

'So how far into the jungle are you taking us?'

'Your guide has told me to land in a clearing about one-hundred and fifty miles from this position. Our ETA should be about eighty minutes.'

Gonzales turned to face Mac. 'Why do you need to know these details? I have arranged everything so that you will have the maximum time on the ground and not too far to walk before we sight any of the animals you wish to see.'

'Yes, I'm sure you have, but we never travel anywhere without knowing where we are going to end up. Has Jorge ever flown you anywhere before?'

'No, we've never met before this morning, Mister Parker.'

'Do you feel dry, Mac?' Sarah said as she took a bottle of water from her haversack.

'Yes, I do.'

'We have water here for passengers,' Pablo called out.

'Thanks, but we're fine. We brought plenty for our needs,' Mac called back.

For the rest of the flight there was little conversation and Mac and Sarah spent the time looking out of the windows at the jungle below.

'I shall be landing in a few minutes,' Jorge called back over his shoulder.

The helicopter started to descend and Jorge positioned it accurately in the middle of a small clearing. He ceased the rotor blades. 'You may now get out,' he said.

'We'll be back at about three-thirty,' Gonzales said.

Jorge and Pablo remained in the helicopter with the windows open while they had a lunch of sandwiches and water.

Gonzales removed his rifle from its canvass case and placed the case on his seat in the helicopter.

'I'll walk at a slow pace, so that you will have time to

look for animals,' he said as he led off with the rifle hanging from its sling over his left shoulder.

Sarah, her eyes peeled for any sightings of animals, had her camera hanging from its strap in front of her. Mac followed closely behind Gonzales.

About half an hour of leaving the helicopter, they had covered about half a mile. Gonzales suddenly turned sharply and levelled his rifle at Mac. Mac and Sarah instinctively froze in their tracks.

'What's this all about? Weren't you ever told that you should never point a gun at anyone unless you intended to shoot them?'

Gonzales gave a menacing laugh. 'You know very well what I want is your fat wallet!'

'Oh, is that what you want? What will you do if I give it to you   shoot me?'

'If you don't hand it over, I shall shoot you and your wife!'

'In that case, I shall let you have it and hope that you are an honourable thief,' Mac said as he reached into his bush jacket and slowly withdrew his arm.

Gonzales took his finger off the trigger and reached out with his right arm to receive the wallet. In a lightning move Mac's hand came out with his pistol and he fired a single shot at the startled face of Gonzales. The bullet entered his head just below his hairline and took off a piece of his skull; he dropped to the ground with blood and brain matter oozing from his head. Mac picked up the automatic rifle and fired two shots into Gonzales's chest, then fired short bursts at the surrounding trees. He took off his bush jacket and fired a single shot at the loose material at the base of the jacket. Turning Gonzales's body over, he went through his pockets. He removed his wallet and a small notebook from his inside pockets.

Sarah, a shocked look on her face, said, 'What was all that about? I know the bastard deserved to die, but why did you shoot him when he was already dead and then fire at those trees and your bush jacket?'

'I am setting the scene for anyone investigating his death. We have been ambushed by a couple of bandits. Gonzales exchanged fire with them and they killed him. The bullet holes in the trees will indicate that there was a brief fire fight. We ran away and they fired after us. That's how I got a hole in my bush jacket. Now the crew will have heard the gunfire and will assume that we've all been killed and may decide to take off in case the bandits find them. So, without further ado we are going to cover that half mile in record speed. Give me the haversack and start running.'

They both started to run.

'Mac, why are you carrying that weapon? It'll slow you down!'

'Don't worry, I'm not taking it far. As soon as we pass some thick bushes I'm going to dump it there. This mustn't be found near the body to provide ballistic testing. But not only that, the bandits wouldn't leave such a useful weapon behind. Now stop nattering and run!'

They arrived at the helicopter site breathless and torn

and bloodied by brambles and low branches. Jorge and Pablo were sitting inside the helicopter; the engine was running and the rotors were whirling.

Mac picked up a piece of fallen branch and beat it against the window. Jorge turned and saw them and cut the engine. Pablo got out and helped them into the helicopter and gave them bottles of water.

'We heard all the shooting and guessed it must have been bandits. We thought you must be dead when the shooting stopped.'

'Yes, we nearly were. Look at the hole in my bush jacket. That was a close call for me. Poor old Gonzales tried to defend us and told us to run while he covered our retreat. The last thing we saw was him dropping dead. The bandits may have been following us so I'd take off as soon as you can.'

'I certainly will,' Jorge said as he switched on the engine. A couple of minutes later the helicopter was airborne and climbing to its normal cruising height.

'I'd better radio the airport to report the murder of your guide,' said Jorge while fiddling with the controls of his radio. 'Damn, it's not working!'

That's good, thought Mac. With me carrying a pistol and Hernando's belongings, we don't want the police meeting us at the airport.

'Don't worry about the radio, Jorge. As soon as we get back, I'll go the police headquarters to report this crime. Of course, they'll want statements from you, so it would be better if you both came with me. If you lose any business because of this, I'll see that you are reimbursed.'

'I understand. As soon as we land I'll get my ground crew to put this baby to bed and come with you to the police headquarters.'

'It might be difficult to pinpoint where we were actually attacked, so it could take days for the police to find Gonzales's body,' Mac said.

Jorge gave a short laugh. 'I don't suppose the police will bother to look for the body. Anyway it's not very likely that it will still be there. The wild cats come out at night and will have dragged it away to be eaten.'

'Oh, how dreadful! Mac, we were lucky not to be supper for wild cats. And I didn't even get any photos!'

'Yes, my dear, it really has been one of those days!'

They made record time back to the airfield. 'Possibly because we had a lighter load,' suggested Mac.

Jorge gave a short laugh and nodded.

After handing over his aircraft Jorge suggested that they have a drink in the airfield canteen before returning to the city. All agreed.

'How much do I owe you for the trip?' Mac said.

Jorge tugged at his beard before answering. 'I was paid the equivalent of seventy-five pounds sterling in advance, so if you're paying in sterling, call it three hundred.'

Mac peeled off six fifty-pound notes and handed them to Jorge.

'Do you want a receipt?' Jorge said.

'No, thanks, Jorge, it's been a pleasure doing business with you.'

'If you're thinking about going to the police headquarters, Mac, might I suggest we return to the hotel first to get cleaned up?' Sarah said with a sly knowing look, which reminded Mac that he should not have a gun, Gonzales's notebook and wallet in his possession when he went to the police headquarters. But he needed to get a translation of the notes in the book.

'Yes, darling, we do need to get washed up and changed before we go to the police. So, if it's all right with you and Pablo, Jorge, come back with us to the hotel and have a meal on us at the hotel while we get cleaned up.'

'Yes, sir, we'd appreciate that. We've never eaten at the Hilton. I'll ring for a taxi.'

The taxi arrived almost immediately and within fifteen minutes they were at the hotel.

Mac caught the eye of the headwaiter and told him that anything the two airmen wanted they could have and the cost of the meal and gratuity should be added to his account.

In their suite Mac and Sarah shared a shower to save time and dressed in their normal clothes. Mac, watched by Sarah, placed the pistol, shoulder holster, spare magazine and Gonzales's wallet in a laundry bag and hung it up under his trench coat in the wardrobe.

'Have you forgotten something, Mac? What about the notebook?'

'No, but it's no use to us if we can't read it. So I'm going to get Hank to get it translated. From what I can make out it contains several addresses in and around Bogotá.'

'But can we trust him?'

'Why not, aren't we on the same side? There's probably information in it that he would like to see.'

Hank was at his desk when they entered the reception area. They caught his eye and he beckoned them over.

'So how was the trip in the jungle?' he said as greeting.

'Very enlightening, in more ways than one,' Mac said withdrawing the notebook from his inside pocket and passing it to Hank. 'Could you get the contents of this notebook translated?'

Hank opened the notebook and glanced at a few of the pages. 'Yes, no problem there. I can do it myself and whatever it contains will then be between us.'

'We're off to the police station to report the murder of our guide Hernando. He was shot by bandits and we were lucky to get away before they got us,' said Mac with a wink.

'Oh, how sad, Hernando will be missed.'

'We should be back in an hour or two. Will that be long enough for you to translate the contents?'

'Sure thing, Mac, you can pick it up when you return. Good luck!'

*   *   *

Mac found Jorge and Pablo waiting near the entrance to the hotel. Jorge led them to a waiting taxi.

'To the police headquarters and please hurry,' said Jorge, who wanted to get the police interview over and go home.

The taxi driver gave a short laugh. 'In this traffic, you must be joking, señor.'

But despite the heavy evening traffic, the driver skilfully weaved his way through slower moving vehicles to reach the police headquarters in what he said was 'record time.'

Mac paid him and added a generous tip.

Inside the police headquarters, Mac addressed the desk sergeant. 'We're here to report a murder!'

The sergeant looked perplexed. Jorge stepped forward and repeated what Mac had said in Spanish. The sergeant immediately went to a telephone and spoke rapidly to whoever had answered. He then turned to Jorge. 'Detective Major Carreras will see you. Please be seated over there,' he said pointing to a row of chairs.

Two or three minutes passed and two stern-faced men approached them. 'Please follow us,' the elder of the two men said in English and led them to a room marked Entravista Cuarto.

'Please be seated. I am Detective Major Carreras and my colleague is Detective Lieutenant Alvarez. Please give me your names and nationalities.' Mac introduced them.

'Now please tell me, Mister Murphy, who has been murdered and where the crime was committed,' said Carreras.

'The victim's name was Hernando Gonzales. He was guiding my wife and me in the jungle when we were attacked by a group of bandits. He tried to defend us and told us to run back to where our helicopter was waiting.

There was a heavy exchange of fire and we saw Hernando hit several times.'

Carreras gave Alvarez a knowing look before he continued. 'How do you know that this man was killed?'

'Because his head was blown open and he was also shot in the chest. We saw that happen before we took flight.'

'What were you doing in the jungle?' Alvarez said.

'We were there to take photographs of the wild life.'

'Weren't you warned about the dangers you might encounter in that area?'

'Yes, but Hernando said we had nothing to fear with him as our guide. He was armed with a sub-machine gun.'

Carreras turned to Jorge. 'Can you give me your actual position when you landed and the direction that the guide led these people?'

Jorge took a piece of paper and wrote something on it and passed it to Carreras.

'What I would like to know is why you didn't radio the airport to tell them about the incident. Had you done so we could have had officers there to meet you and saved a lot of time.'

Jorge reddened under his beard. 'Yes, Major, I'm sorry about that, but my radio went unserviceable. That's the first time that has ever happened in any plane I've piloted.'

'Yes, it was rather unfortunate, happening when it did.'

Turning to Mac, Carreras said: 'Did the bandits follow you, Mister Murphy?'

'For a short distance, I believe. They fired after us and

they shot a hole in my bush jacket. But aside from that we got back to the helicopter, scratched and breathless after running half a mile through the jungle.'

'You were extremely lucky, Mister Murphy, to have got away from these men. There have been many cases of foreigners being kidnapped and held for ransom, or even robbed and killed for whatever of value they had.'

'Yes, Major Carreras, we appreciate that and will not be making that trip again.'

'How long do you intend to remain in this country?'

'Well, we haven't really thought about a date for leaving. We have open tickets and hoped to remain here to see as much as we can of your delightful and interesting country,' Mac replied tongue in cheek.

'You are all now free to go, but we might wish to see you again, Mister Murphy, so you must report to this office before you leave Bogotá.'

'Thank you, Major, Lieutenant,' said Mac as he led their party out of the office and on to the street to hail two taxis.

Back in the police headquarters Carreras and Alvarez were elated. 'What a bit of luck, we've got rid of that thug, Gonzales,' said Carrerras. 'We've been after him for years and fate steps in and we can write him off our wanted list.'

'So, you don't want to follow up on what we've learnt from those two English nitwits?'

'No, forget them. There's nothing to investigate and the big cats will get rid of Gonzales's remains.'

*   *   *

Back at the hotel, Mac and Sarah went to Hank's desk. He was reading through the notebook and making notes in another notebook.

Hank handed Mac a sheaf of notes. 'You've certainly got hold of some useful intelligence, Mac, and we've already made good use of it.'

'What have you done?'

'You'll read about it in tomorrow's newspaper. But what you've got here is also the addresses in and around Bogotá where they're holding your film-makers.'

'Thanks a million, Hank. This mission might prove a lot easier than I thought. We'll start calling on them tomorrow.'

'Hold your horses, Mac! Don't underestimate the people you're up against. They'd cut your throat for a sawbuck!'

'What's a sawbuck, Hank?'

'I'm sorry, Sarah, I forgot you don't savvy US English. It's a ten-dollar bill,' replied Hank, with a laugh. He went on: 'I've made a copy of your notebook, Mac, so here is yours back. My translations are on those sheets. From what I've read about Señor Gonzales, the world is a safer place without him.'

'Yes, I have to agree with you there. We'll say goodnight, Hank. My gammy leg is playing up from all the running about we've had today and Sarah nearly fell asleep in the taxi.'

'Goodnight, Mac, Sarah.'

CHAPTER NINE

23 MARCH

While he and Sarah were eating their room-service breakfast, Mac scanned the newspapers to see if there was anything reported about what Hank had said would be in the morning papers. Whatever had happened must have occurred after the newspapers had been put to bed.

Sarah switched the television on to the news channel. A breaking news item revealed that there had been an explosion in a building in the outer suburbs of Bogotá. The building was purported to be a small factory manufacturing cushions and pillows. But police and fire officers who attended the burning building found that it contained a large amount of coca, which was being processed into cocaine. The police claimed that a number of arrests had been made.

'So, that's what Hank was talking about. He must have got the address of the factory from Hernando's notebook. The CIA certainly hit pay dirt when they read the late unlamented Hernando's notebook.'

'Yes, a coup for the CIA, but what about the people *we're* looking for?' Sarah said.

'I have the location of two of the hostages.' Mac waved one of the sheets of paper that Hank had given him.

'Well, what are we going to do   crash into where they are with guns drawn and demand their release? Surely you'll need a recce of the place before we try anything like that?'

'Of course, we would, but first I'm going to let Lionel know what we've got.'

'Do you want me with you?'

'No, there's a more pressing job that needs to be done. Phone Hugo and ask him if he's got the tools we need to do our work. If he has, ask him to have them delivered here. That means one of us must remain in the suite until they arrive.'

'All right, if that's what you want. If you leave the translations, I'll check the position of any other addresses they reveal and mark them on our map of Bogotá and area.'

'That's my girl! We'll certainly need those locations,' Mac said as he left the sitting room.

He tapped on Durrance's door, which was almost immediately opened by Madge.

'Good morning, Madge. Is his Lordship up yet?'

'Yes, he's out on the balcony eating his breakfast.'

'Good, I have something important to tell him. So, take me to your leader.'

Madge led him through the sitting room and out on to the balcony.

Durrance put a forkful of scrambled egg back on his plate before he spoke. 'I hope it's some good news you have to impart.'

'Yes, it is, Lionel. I have obtained a personal notebook

that once belonged to that treacherous guide who led your people into an ambush. The book contains several addresses with remarks written under them. These have been translated and in one or two cases locations show that members of your party are being held there.'

'That's splendid news, Mac. Give me the addresses and I'll get on to the police to raid the houses!'

'If that's what you want. It's your party, but this operation must be carried out secretly, because if those holding the hostages are able to contact their leader before the rescue has been made and the kidnappers arrested, Moretta will move all the other abductees to different locations.'

'Yes, of course, that's the way it must be done.'

Mac handed him the sheet with one of the addresses on it.

Durrance read the details. 'I see that this is the address of where Jasper Maybrick and Danny Bristow are being held.'

'Is Maybrick one of the supporting actors and Bristow a cameraman?' Mac said, to show that he had a good memory for names.

'Yes, that's right, and they should be celebrating their freedom in this hotel tonight." He shouted into the sitting room: 'Madge! Get onto the chief of police and tell him what we've got and ask him, very politely, to send a detective officer to collect the information we're holding.'

'Right, boss!' Madge shouted back.

'By the way, Mac, you haven't told me how you acquired the notebook from that guide.'

'No, because it's a very long story and I'd rather not say anything more than that he won't be misguiding anyone again. Cheerio for now, Lionel, I'll be in touch.' Mac walked back into the sitting room to see Madge talking to the chief of police on the phone. He gave her a wave and left the room.

*   *   *

Mac and Sarah kept the television news channel on all day, hoping that any attempt to rescue two hostages would not be publicized. It was early evening when a breaking news item reported that Groupo de Accion per la Libertad Personal (United Action Group to Rescue Kidnap Victims) had stormed a large detached house in the northern suburbs of Bogotá, in an attempt to rescue two British film company employees. Unfortunately, the two kidnapped Britons were shot in the crossfire between the rescue group and the kidnappers. There were believed to be four kidnappers in the house, three of whom were killed. Four members of the rescue group were also killed. A spokesman for the Defence Ministry stated that military and police units were conducting a nationwide search for the remainder of the kidnapped Britons.

'Damn, damn!' Mac almost shouted as he turned off the television. 'That's *exactly* what I didn't want to happen. Moretta now knows what happened and will almost certainly move the kidnapped film-makers to new locations.'

'So, what are you going to do now, have a row with him next door?' Sarah said.

'I'll certainly give him a piece of my mind.'

'You can't really blame him entirely for what went wrong. I'm sure he would have asked the authorities to deal very discreetly. But you know how police operations are leaked to the media. Although in this case I'd have thought that with their operation being such a disaster, they would have wanted to keep a lid on it. Anyway, what do you propose to do now?'

'I must try to locate at least one of their safe houses before the hostages are moved.'

'Do you think our friendly CIA man might help in any way? You did give him some information that proved very useful for him.'

'I know, but he is only a section leader and wouldn't have sufficient authority to get embroiled in something outside his responsibility. But I'll try him, he might be able to suggest a way I can keep tabs on the kidnappers' movements.'

'Are you going down to see him now? If you are I'd better stay up here in case Hugo or one of his people turns up with our tools.'

'Yes, you'd better. I'll get back as soon as I can. And as soon as we get the delivery we'll go down to dinner. If someone turns up with the goods while I'm downstairs, ring the concierge's phone. I want to return Hugo's things.'

'Okay, darling, I'll see you later,' said Sarah and turned the television on.

Hank was at his desk reading and looked up when Mac approached. 'Come into my office.' Mac followed him into the office and sat down.

'That was certainly tough luck, the Colombian Special Services outfit fouling up their mission. No doubt Moretta will try to get the rest of the hostages moved to new locations.'

'That's what I've come to see you about. Have you any idea how I can find out where they may move.'

'After what you did for us I'd like to do you a favour in return. But I'm sure you are aware of the constraints placed on my actions.'

'Sure, Hank, I had similar rules and regulations to follow in the SAS and if there's nothing you can do to help, I quite understand.'

'There is one thing I could do without compromising my position. I have five officers in my section and I could assign them to watch the one other address where two of the film-makers are being held. I can tell my men to photograph everyone who enters and leaves the house. They will assume that I am trying to track the movements of members of the drug cartels. And when anyone leaves the house and drives to a new location they will follow and report to me and I'll pass the address to you. How does that sound, Mac?'

'That's ideal for my purpose. If I can nail one of the kidnappers I can persuade him to give me details of the other locations. How soon can you put your idea into action, Hank?'

'I can do it now, Mac,' he said taking his copy of Hernando's notebook from his desk drawer. 'I'll ring a couple of my people and get them started tonight. They can work a shift system and cover the two buildings until they get the info you want.'

'Thanks a million, Hank. If you can take a couple of hours off from your desk tonight, I'd like to invite you to have dinner with Sarah and me.'

'Yes, I'd like that.'

'So as not to compromise you in any way, we'll have the meal in our suite. Come up in about thirty minutes and bring a couple of Room Service menus with you.'

The dinner lasted a lot longer than two hours and Hank proved to have the same liking and capacity for Remy Martin as Mac.

Hank kept his cell phone switched on and a little before midnight the message they had all been hoping to hear came through. One of Hank's men had photographed a group of about six people getting into a black van. He sent his colleague to follow the vehicle. Twenty minutes later he reported back that the group had entered a large house about twelve miles east from where they had started. He gave his colleague the address of the house and it was passed on to Hank, who wrote it down on his napkin and passed it to Mac.

'It looks as though we got that address in the nick of time, Mac; if we'd delayed the operation until tomorrow morning it would have been too late to get their new location.'

'Yes, that was a great piece of intelligence work in the field, which is much appreciated,' said Mac as he refilled their glasses.

'No more for me, Mac,' cried Sarah. 'If we are going after that group tomorrow we'd better get some rest. By the way, I didn't mention it earlier because I didn't want us to be talking about guns all night, but while you were out, Hugo sent a courier with our necessaries.'

'Did you give the courier Hugo's property?'

'Yes, and told him to tell Hugo that it had been used to good effect.'

'Well, Hank, you heard what my boss said; we've got to get some shut-eye.'

'Okay, I can take a hint and I don't think I'll have much trouble dropping off tonight,' said Hank, muffling a yawn with his hand. 'Goodnight, Mac, Sarah.'

'Goodnight, Hank, and thanks again for what you did for me and the British Film Industry.'

As soon as Hank had left the room, Sarah went into the bedroom and brought back a large canvas satchel. It was locked.

'Did the courier bring a key?'

'Yes, here it is,' said Sarah, handing him a sealed envelope with Hugo's recognizable signature on the back of the envelope.

'Those MI6 boys really revel in cloak and dagger stuff,' said Mac as he tore open the envelope and took out a key. He opened the satchel and removed its contents   two Glock 18 automatic pistols, two sound moderators, two shoulder holsters, six fully loaded spare magazines and a box of a hundred 9 mm Parabellum cartridges.

'Hmm…252 rounds of ammo   enough to start a small war,' Mac said as he replaced the items in the haversack. 'Right, it's off to bed now for four hours' sleep. We must arrive early and catch them all while they're still groggy. They will have had a very late night settling into their new location.'

'Have you given any thought as to how we are going to tackle this operation, Mac?'

'No, it's one of those situations when you have to play it by ear.'

'Play it by ear   is that another of your illogical phrases?'

'Yes, Sarah. The logic of it will become apparent to you tomorrow.'

CHAPTER TEN

24 MARCH

Mac woke Sarah at 4 a.m. 'Never mind showering and breakfast. That can wait until we return. We can get coffee in the reception area. It's available all night.'

'So you expect to be back very soon, when you haven't a clue of what we might have to contend with?'

Mac didn't reply but opened the haversack. 'Here's a gun for you, a spare magazine, shoulder holster and a silencer. Fix it to the gun, now.'

Sarah placed the items on the bed. 'What shall we wear?'

'Just our jungle gear and scarves to cover our faces; we can't afford to be seen by the kidnappers.'

Mac quickly dressed, fitted his silencer to his pistol, holstered the gun and slipped two spare magazines into his bush jacket pocket. Opening his bedside unit drawer he took out a lead-filled and leather-covered sap and slipped it into his hip pocket. The weapon was a souvenir of his time in Iraq, when he had worked with a US special services unit.

'What are you taking that for, Mac? We could be up against automatic weapons!'

'We may need to put some people back to sleep when

we arrive. It's a great little sleep inducer,' Mac said with a laugh.

Sarah, fully dressed, sat on the end of the bed watching Mac as he took a long length of thin, but strong, cord from his suitcase and wound it around his waist under his bush jacket.

'You're not thinking of hanging the kidnappers, are you?'

'No, but it's always handy to have a length of rope in your armoury.'

'Are you ready now?'

'Yes, darling', Mac answered looking at his watch. 'We've got fifteen minutes to drink a cup of coffee before our hired car arrives.'

They drank and went out onto the dark and near deserted street.

A large black Mercedes drove up to the kerb and stopped in front of them. The driver turned down the window and looked at them. 'Are you Mac and Sarah?'

'Yes, and who are you?' Mac asked.

'You can call me Bart, short for Bartolo. Hank sent me. I'm to take you wherever you want to go.'

'You're not a CIA man, are you?'

'No, I do all sort of odd jobs for Hank. It's one way of making a living, without being employed by the drug cartels,' Bart replied with a wry smile.

'Good, I'll give you the address when we get into the car.' Mac opened the side door behind the driver. 'You get in there, Sarah, and I'll sit next to Bart.' Mac walked around the car, got in and sat next to Bart. Mac took a piece of paper from his pocket and handed it to Bart, who read aloud the address: '54 Calle 72, in the Los Ferias Occidental area. I know it well,' said Bart as he handed the paper back to Mac before he put the car into gear and drove swiftly away from the kerb.

'How long will it take to get there, Bart?'

'At this time in the morning, not more than ten minutes.'

'Good. When we enter Calle 72, stop a few doors away from number 54. You might see a large van parked outside that house. Stay parked behind it, ready to move off at very short notice.'

'Sure thing, skipper.'

Within ten minutes Bart stopped about ten yards from the large van. Mac and Sarah got out of the car and walked to the van.

'How are we going to play this, Mac?'

'I'll ring the doorbell and as soon as the door is opened have your pistol ready, but not in view. The rest will be up to me to play it by ear!'

The door to the house was on the same level as the pavement. Mac pressed the doorbell. There was a delay of about a minute before the door was slowly opened and a tall, bearded man, dressed in blue denim, stood in the doorway. Before he could speak, Mac said, 'Hola buenos dias, señor. Habla usted ingles?'

The man glowered suspiciously at Mac and said: 'Yes, I speak the ingles. What do you want, calling at this hour of the morning?'

Mac nudged Sarah's elbow and she moved aside and prodded the man in the stomach with her pistol. 'Make the slightest sound and you're dead!' Sarah said in a low but menacing voice.

A sap appeared in Mac's right hand and he struck the man either side of his head. The man slid unconscious to the floor.

Mac removed an automatic pistol from the man's hip pocket and put it in a side pocket of his bush jacket. He unwound about two yards of the cord around his waist and cut it with a pocket knife. He turned the man over, face down on the carpet, pulled his arms backwards and tied his hands together, then lifted the man's legs up his back and slipped his tied arms over his legs. Next, he took off the man's shoes and socks and rammed one of the socks into his mouth.

'That should keep him quiet until we've finished upstairs,' Mac whispered, as he led the way up the stairs.

'The first thing we must do is to locate the hostages. You stay on the landing and if any of the kidnappers appear, take the necessary action   shoot them!'

There were four doors on the landing. Three bedrooms and a bathroom, Mac surmised.

Loud sounds of snoring came from one room. Mac quietly opened one of the other doors and peered into the room. It was devoid of any furniture, or sleeping bodies. He closed the door and went to the other room. The room was unfurnished, but afforded by dawn's early light he saw a fully dressed man tied to a radiator pipe. He crept over to the man, who immediately awoke. Mac placed his hand over the man's mouth and whispered: 'Don't speak above a whisper. I'm here to rescue you. I expected to find two of you – where is the other hostage?'

The man struggled to sit up. 'The bastards killed Martin Walters.'

'We'll talk about that later, but first I must free you,' said Mac, as he started to cut through the ropes. When the man was free and rubbing his wrists, he said, 'My name is Harry Franklin,'

'The film director?'

'Yes, that's right. But who are you?'

'Just call me Mac. I've been hired to rescue your film party. But enough of that now; what I want to know is how many bandits are there in the building?'

'I believe there are four. Three sleep on the floor next door and one other stays awake as a guard. I don't know where he is.'

'He's sleeping on the doormat. How are they armed?'

'They all have automatic rifles and pistols.'

'Can you handle a pistol, Harry?'

'Yes, I was drafted before the first Iraq war, infantry trained and was made a lieutenant and commanded a platoon. I…'

'Sorry, we've no time for your military history,' Mac said, thrusting the guard's pistol into Harry's hand.

'Now listen, Harry, this is what we're going to do. My partner is on the landing covering us if those kidnappers wake up. We're going to enter the room, disarm them and tie them all up and put them in that van outside.'

'Why not just shoot them as they sleep? They've murdered at least five of our company.'

'No, I don't do things like that and anyway I have other plans for them. I shall cover them with my silenced pistol and you will remove their weapons.'

Mac led Harry out onto the landing. 'This is Sarah, my wife, Harry. No more introductions now, though.'

Mac entered the room and switched on the electric light. The three men were fully clothed and partially covered with blankets. They stirred and rubbed their eyes.

'Make one move to pick up your weapons and you're dead!' Mac shouted.

One man pulled a pistol from under his blanket, but before he could fire it, Mac put a bullet through his upper arm. The man screamed in pain.

'If any of you try to do that again you'll get a bullet through your head. Harry, collect their weapons but don't get between them and me. And while you're at it get them to empty all their pockets and pile their content next to the door.'

'Okay, Mac, I know the drill.'

Sarah entered the room and levelled her pistol at the three men on the floor.

'Now get up and stand facing that wall and put your hands behind you back,' Sarah ordered.

Harry demonstrated the position for the benefit of those who didn't understand English.

When Mac had tied the hands of each man he linked them together by tying the cord around the first man's head and looping it around the heads of the other two.

'Now, who's got the keys to the van? Don't keep me waiting for an answer!' Mac shouted and prodded each man in the back with his pistol.

'They're on a shelf in the bathroom,' one of the men blurted out.

Sarah went into the bathroom and returned with a small bunch of keys and gave them to Mac.

'Harry, lead them downstairs and hold them in the passage,' Mac said.

'What about the weapons I've collected, Mac?'

'Keep the handguns, unload the automatic rifles; they can be put into the van with our prisoners.'

When they were all downstairs, Mac opened the front door and walked to the van. One of the keys opened the rear door.

'Bring them over here, Harry, and get them into the van.'

'This one's still unconscious,' Sarah said, pointing to the man on the hall floor.

Mac went into the kitchen and filled a plastic bowl that was in the sink, with water. Returning to the hall he pulled the sock out of the man's mouth and poured the water over his head. The man came to spluttering and mouthing oaths.

'Hold him here until Harry comes for him while I collect their belongings in this bowl,' said Mac as he went back up the stairs.

When the fourth man was in the van and secured to the other three, Mac locked the door.

Bart had got out of his vehicle to watch what was happening. 'What are you going to do now, Mac?'

I'd like you to drive to the police headquarters. I'll follow you in the van. When I get there I shall leave the van parked near the police headquarters and join you in the car. I want you to then take me to the nearest telephone kiosk. Are you all right with that?'

'Yeah, no problem; there's a public phone box a few hundred yards from the police headquarters. You can ring the emergency police number, which is 123.'

'Sarah, you and Harry get in the car,' Mac said and handed her the bowl of items he had taken from the kidnappers.

When they arrived at the police headquarters Mac stopped the van behind the car, which Bart had driven a few yards past the main entrance to police headquarters. Mac got out of the van and got into the car.

Bart turned the car around to the way they had come and drove to the telephone kiosk. Mac got out of the car and entered the kiosk. He dialled 123. A guttural voice answered in Spanish. Mac replied, 'Policia habla usted ingles?'

There was a brief pause and the voice said, 'Yes, what do you want?'

'I am reporting that there is a van parked outside the police headquarters. In the van there are four of Moretta's banditos who kidnapped a number of British film company employees. There are also automatic weapons in the van, but they are not loaded. Do you fully understand what I have said?'

'Si, señor, but what is your name?'

'Never mind my name, just arrest the men in the van before they break loose.'

Mac replaced the phone and got back in the car. 'Home, Bart, and don't spare the horses!'

*   *   *

Back at the hotel Mac gave Bart a generous bonus.

'Many thanks, Mac, but Hank has already paid me for this trip.'

'Never mind that; this is for your honesty. I might want to use your services again, so have you a business card?'

Bart took a card from his wallet. 'You can always contact me on this number,' he said handing Mac the card.

'Chao, Mac,' Bart said as he got into his car and drove away from the hotel at high speed.

Mac gave Bart a wave as he disappeared from view.

'Right, let's visit Lionel now and see if he's up yet,' said Mac, leading them to the lift. As they entered the lift Mac glanced across the reception area to the concierge's desk. Hank wasn't there. Probably plotting CIA business in his office, thought Mac.

A fully dressed Madge answered Mac's tap on the door. 'Yes, Mac, the boss is up, dressed and having breakfast and eager for your report. I see you've been successful in rescuing Harry. Lionel will be pleased. You all look a bit jaded, particularly you, Harry.'

'I certainly am. I haven't had any proper food or sleep since we were kidnapped.'

'I'll get room service to bring up three full English breakfasts,' Madge said.

'Bring them all out here, Madge,' Durrance shouted from the balcony.

'It's good to see you, Harry.' said Durrance, 'I thought we'd lost you. What happened to Martin Walters? I know he has been killed – I had another letter from Moretta.'

'I'm afraid it's bad news, Lionel. A couple of nights ago, I think   I've lost track of time   Martin and I were tied to metal rings fixed to the wall, when two of Moretta's men came into the room. One of them grabbed Martin by the hair and the other cut his throat. All I could do was to lie there and witness the horror of their act. I thought it would be unwise to say anything that might cause them to do the same to me. They cut him free and dragged his body from the room.'

'How dreadful!' Sarah gasped. 'Why would they do that when they said that the hostages would be safe, until the end of March?'

'I received a letter from Moretta yesterday. It had been left at reception for me. He wrote that he had Martin killed in revenge for the killing of his men by the special services unit. He also stated that as he had now lost three of his hostages the ransom money for them would be added to that for the remaining hostages. He gave the account number for the money to be paid into the Bank of Panama. I also have some good news to tell you. The CEO of Omega Films has been negotiating with the Brazilian film industry and Brazil's Minister of the Interior, which has led to an agreement that when we have secured the release of our people we can finish our film in the Brazilian jungle, a few miles southeast of Colombia's border. The area is safe and inhabited by a tribe of friendly natives, who would be willing to act as extras in our film.'

'That's certainly good news, Lionel, but we still have to raise the money to pay the ransoms that we need to free our people,' Harry said.

'That matter is in hand and with a bit of luck we may yet raise what we need from donations and loans. However, I should like to hear what Mac has to say about the progress he is making.'

Before Mac could say a word, the room service waiters arrived with their breakfasts.

'If it is okay with you, Lionel, I'll deliver my debriefing after we've all had a hearty breakfast.'

'Yes, of course, go ahead, enjoy it. It looks so good I'm almost tempted to have another.'

*　　*　　*

'Major, I've received a message from the control room sergeant that a van containing four of Moretta's men has been left outside the headquarters,' Lieutenant Barbosa said excitedly.

Major Estrada glowered at Barbosa. 'Well, what have you done about it?'

'It's all very strange, so I thought I ought to report it to you straight away.'

'What's strange about it?'

'The control room received an anonymous call from a foreigner, an Englishman, he thought. He said that the van had four of Moretta's men inside and that there were also weapons in the van.'

The major suddenly looked worried. 'That is rather strange. Don't let anyone go near the van and have barriers put across the road to restrict traffic. I'll consult the colonel and let you know what to do later.' After a moment he got through to the colonel.

'Sorry to bother you, sir, but there is a vehicle parked quite near the front entrance of the building. It has been anonymously reported that the vehicle contains four of that Brigand Moretta's men. I think that this is some sort of booby trap that Moretta would plan and that the vehicle contains explosives that will be set off if we try to open the doors or to move it away.'

'Has anyone tried to open the doors, Major?'

'No, sir, strict instructions have been given that no one is to go near the van and I've instructed the duty officer to have road blocks put up to stop through traffic.'

'I suppose we ought to call out the Bomb Squad to check it, but that could take time and it won't be long before the street will be filled with people going to work. We must neutralize it as soon as possible. But before we do that have all the blast shutters put up at the windows at the front of the building.'

'How do we neutralize it? We don't have appropriate explosives immediately available to organize a controlled explosion of the vehicle.'

'Detail six men to put on flak jackets and helmets and have them armed with the heaviest weapons we have in the armoury. Deploy three men behind each barrier. Radio the fire chief and tell him to position two fire engines behind the barriers. When that has been done detail a man to fire a flare from an upper window. That is the signal for your six men to open up with rapid and continuous fire at all surfaces of the vehicle. If there are explosives in the vehicle they will soon be exploded. There will be fuel in the vehicle which will ignite. When that happens, the fire crews can soon douse the flames. Have you any questions, Major?'

'Well…er…I was just wondering if the anonymous caller was right about the van being occupied by Moretta's men, sir.'

'If that was true, it would surely be a good way to rid us of some of those accursed left-wing bandits! Now get things moving!'

'Yes, sir,' Estrada replied as he almost ran from the office.

*   *   *

'What an extraordinary account, Mac. You made it sound like something extracted from a Boys' Own Weekly,' Durrance said. 'What are your plans now?'

'Sarah and I are going to examine all the kidnappers' effects that we took from them. We might find something that'll give us a clue as to where the other members of your company are being held.'

'Let's hope you do find something useful, because we've only got six more days left before the kidnappers carry out their threat to start killing the hostages.'

'Okay, Lionel, we'll go back to work in our suite and return as soon as we find anything to put us on the right track. I should turn on your television. There might be some interesting news reports coming through later today.'

'Yes, I'll do that. See you later, Mac.'

Back in their suite, Mac tipped the contents of the plastic bowl onto their bed.

'We'll empty all their wallets first and look for business cards and any documents, maps or letters which might contain addresses of where the hostages are being held.'

'What about the money? There seems to be quite a lot,' Sarah said as she started to empty the wallets.

'That'll help defray our expenses,' Mac replied with a grin.

'I see there are a couple of small notebooks among the stuff. Of course, all the notes are in Spanish. Shall we get Hank to translate them for us?'

'Yes, we'll take them to him when we go down for lunch.'

'What about all the other unidentifiable oddments, such as cigarettes, lighters, penknives, pornographic photographs, condoms and what looks like ecstasy pills?' Sarah said, piling the items on a chair.

'We'll put them in one of the landing rubbish bins on the way down.'

'What about driving licences?'

'We'll keep them. They could come in useful. Perhaps Hank could use them if he wanted any of his people to take on another identity.'

'This is an interesting coincidence, Mac; all four of those men seem to belong to the same club. It's described as the El Fantastico Club!'

Mac took the card. 'Yes, but this may be more than a coincidence. It could be a regular haunt for the Moretta bunch. This place might be worth a visit.'

'What would you hope to gain by going there? I know we, or rather just you, could probably be able to bluff your way in with one of these cards. But not speaking the language would be a handicap to gathering any intelligence.'

'That's true, Sarah, but I wouldn't try to pass myself off as a local, but as a tourist who had found a wallet belonging to the owner of the club card and wanted to return the property to Señor Javier Gallardo,' Mac said, reading the name on the card. 'I would tell the manager of the club that as the wallet contained a considerable amount of money I did not wish losing it to some street mugger, so would he let me have Gallardo's address and I would arrange to go there, with an escort, to return the wallet.'

'When do you intend to go there? To avoid the chance of one of Gallardo's pals being there, it would be better to go outside the normal opening times.'

'I couldn't agree more, Sarah. I'll go early tomorrow before the club opens and hope that the manager, or someone with access to the club's records, lives on the premises.'

'Well, having settled that, Mac, let's go down for lunch and call on Hank with the documents for him to translate.'

Hank was at his desk and Mac handed him the documents and letters to him with a knowing wink.

'We're going for a quick meal, so we'll see you later. Tell me, Hank, do you have any information about a club called El Fantastico?'

Hank gave an almost inaudible whistle. 'If the Devil casts his net there, he'd get a good haul of followers! You're not thinking of going there, are you?'

'Yes, but outside opening times.'

'You'll have to make it very early in the morning, because the joint's open from ten in the morning to about three a.m. next day.'

'That's what I intend to do. Is there anyone in the club after it closes?'

'Yes, the owner, Almondo Zamarco; he has a luxury apartment above the club. The entrance to it is a side door to the club. A word of warning – watch your step, Mac, he's a real son-of-a-bitch, who'd have your throat cut for speaking out of turn!'

'Thanks for the info, Hank, I'll take your advice; cheerio for now.'

Before Hank could answer, a hotel resident buttonholed him for information about theatre tickets.

Mac and Sarah, anxious to get back to see what was on the television news, had a hurried lunch and went to Durrance's suite. Madge let them in. Durrance and Franklin were watching television. Durrance turned to them when they entered the room. 'You missed the best news I've heard in ages!' he said excitedly.

'Then share it with us, Lionel,' Mac said, as he and Sarah made themselves comfortable on an ornate sofa.

Durrance turned the television off. 'We've been watching a breaking news report from the police headquarters. It's been repeated all morning. The police chief announced that a heavily-armed group of Moretta's men had attempted to blow up the police headquarters by parking an explosive filled vehicle at the front of the building. Fortunately, the explosive device failed. The insurgents then attacked the headquarters with automatic weapons and hand grenades, but were quickly repelled by the rapid reaction of officers who were in the building at the time. In the ensuing fire-fight four of the attackers were killed. There were no police casualties. The police chief went on to commend the fire service for their rapid and successful action in extinguishing the blazing vehicle, which had exploded when stray bullets hit the petrol tank and was a great danger to members of the public. The police chief ended his report by promising that he would be ordering an immediate crackdown on insurgent groups and appealed to the public to support the police by informing them of any sightings of known members of the insurgent groups responsible for acts of terrorism and violence.'

'That was certainly a great piece of PR by the police,' Mac said with a laugh.

'Yes, they took full advantage of the way you set them

up, Mac,' Durrance said. 'Harry has filled me in with your operation that freed him. Congratulations to you and Sarah. What's your next move?'

'We'll be following up on some information we found on the kidnappers. I'll let you know the result. By the way, will you be sending Harry to Brazil to prepare the way for your film crew?'

'Yes, that's what I had in mind,' Durrance said.

'Hey, just a minute, boss! Don't I have a say in the matter?' Franklin cried. 'Hadn't we better wait to see how many of our company survive? We've already lost an actor, a cameraman, our security officer and my assistant director. Not to mention three local porters. My recommendation is that we ask Omega Films to earmark replacements and when our people are back on the scene and rested, move into the new location in Brazil. But aside from all that I feel I have a responsibility to help Mac with his mission.'

'Well, it is, of course, your decision, Lionel, but Harry proved himself very useful in carrying out the mission. In addition he is an ex-combat infantry officer. He also speaks a little Spanish. So, I'd be glad to have him at my left hand in future rescue operations.'

'Okay, Mac, he is now under your command, but he is very valuable to Omega Films, so make sure you take good care of him.'

'We will, Lionel, don't worry, we will,' Mac replied with a laugh.

CHAPTER ELEVEN

25 MARCH

Franklin joined Mac and Sarah for an early breakfast in their suite.

'Do you want me to come with you on this visit to El Fantastico, Mac?'

'No, this visit is best done alone. You and Sarah can spend some more time in gathering information from that material we took from the kidnappers. Another job you can do is to buy some more suitable clothing than you are wearing. Sarah will take you. Don't worry about money; we have an expense account, provided by the kidnappers. When you return from your shopping expedition, Harry, stay here. I don't know how long I'll be. It'll depend on how I make out with Señor Almondo Zamarco. By the way, have you still got that pistol I gave you?'

'I certainly have,' Franklin said, pulling it out from his belt. 'I've also got three spare magazines.'

'That's great, because you may get to use it later today.'

Mac strapped on his shoulder holster, holstered his pistol and put the sound moderator and a spare magazine in the inside pockets of his bush jacket.'

'Take care, darling,' said Sarah as she followed Mac to the door. 'Please don't take any unnecessary risks.'

'Don't worry my dear, I'll only do what I have to do,' Mac said taking her into his arms and kissing her.

After Mac left, Franklin started to sort through the documents.

'I don't expect we'll find anything we haven't checked before,' Sarah said. 'I suspect Mac gave us that job to take our minds off what we might have to face before this job is over.'

'I can see that you and Mac are very much in love, but can't understand why he exposes you to such danger,' Franklin said.

Sarah gave a little laugh. 'Danger is what keeps us together. You've probably not been told about our backgrounds and what we've been through together since we first met. Mac was a retired captain in the SAS on holiday with his family in Morocco when a car bomb exploded outside Rick's place in Casablanca, killing his wife and two children and severely injuring him. He nearly lost his left leg and still suffers from his injuries. I was a captain in the Israeli Secret Service at the time and my colonel persuaded Mac to help us find the terrorists, who Mac had seen just before the explosion. These terrorists were bent on disrupting the peace talks then taking place between the Israeli Government and the Palestinians. When Mac recovered he joined us and it was through his subsequent actions that the entire group, known as the "*El Mahdi itnayn we itnashar*" (The Mahdi twelve), were eliminated and the talks were saved, though not for long. I doubt that a solution will ever be found for a peaceful resettlement of the Palestinian people. We also worked together with the Syrian insurgents in rescuing a British journalist and his wife.'

Franklin looked awestruck. 'What a pair of intrepid adventurers you are! I could make a film about what you've just told me. Have either of you ever done any acting?'

Sarah tossed back her head and laughed. 'When we're in action we're acting a lot braver than we really are!'

*   *   *

Mac paid the taxi driver through the car's window and walked to the side entrance of the club. He pressed the doorbell and waited. A full minute passed before the door was opened by a short, overweight, swarthy-faced man of about forty.

He looked Mac up and down before he spoke in Spanish: 'Yes, what is your business with Señor Zamarco?'

Mac answered with his limited Spanish, 'Buenos Dias, Señor, habla usted inglesi?'

'Yes, I speak English,' he replied.

'My name is Paul Smurthwaite. I'm a British tourist and I wish to speak to Señor Almondo Zamarco, who I believe is the owner of this club.'

'Yes, Señor Zamarco is the owner, but he is a very busy man. So, tell me what you wish to speak about and I'll see if he will see you.'

'I have found some valuable property of a member of this club and want to see that it is safely returned to him.'

'What is the name of the member?'

'The name on his membership card, which I found with his property, is Javier Gallardo.'

'Have you the property with you? If you have, give it to me and I'll see that he receives it next time he visits the club.'

'No, that is why I wish to speak with the Señor Zamarco.'

The man scowled, 'Oh, very well, I'll check if my boss will see you.'

He took a cell phone from his jacket pocket, pressed one number and muttered a few words in Spanish and listened for an answer.

'Señor Zamarco will see you. Follow me,' he said leading Mac to a lift at the end of the passage.

The lift passed two floors and stopped. The door opened and the man crossed the passage to a door opposite the lift. He tapped on the door and it swung open, presumably done by remote control by the occupant of the room. The man led Mac into the large, but sparsely furnished office. There were two easy chairs, an occasional table, a filing cabinet, a wall safe, and a huge desk. Apart from a lamp, a blotter, a notepad and ornate telephone, the desk was bare.

Almondo Zamarco, sallow faced, slit-eyed, heavy featured, with a closely shaved head of black hair and a thin scar on the side of his left cheek, looked up as Mac entered. It looked like a duelling scar, but Mac guessed it to be the result of a knife fight in the man's youth. He motioned Mac to sit down.

'Raul, you remain.' Raul took up a position next to the door.

Zamarco looked down at his notepad before he spoke. 'I understand that your name is Paul Smurthwaite and that you are a British tourist, who has found some property belonging to Javier Gallardo, a member of my club. How did you know he was a member of this club?'

'I found a club card in his wallet. There were also some papers and a considerable amount of Colombian and US currency in the wallet.'

'Have you the wallet with you? If you have I can have it delivered to Gallardo's home.'

'No, I'm afraid not. I have to admit that I am in a rather weakened state recovering from war wounds and am suffering from post-traumatic stress syndrome resulting from my experiences in Afghanistan, so I thought it prudent not to carry a large sum of money in an area where I might become the victim of a mugging.'

'You seem to be a very honest man, Mister Smurthwaite, so I find it rather strange that you didn't hand the wallet to a police officer, but are going to a lot of trouble to return it to its rightful owner. Unlike you, most people would have pocketed the money and thrown the wallet away.'

'Yes, I suppose you are right there, Señor Zamarco, but I have to say that I have little faith in the honesty of your police and have been brought up to believe that honesty is always the best policy.'

Zamarco tried to smile, but produced a sneering look. 'You are quite right not to trust our police. Regretfully, there is much corruption in the country. So, if I do give you the address, which is in a very dangerous area for tourists to visit, will you feel safe to carry all that money?'

Mac put on worried look. 'No, but I will arrange for a hotel employee to accompany me.'

'Hmm…you might have some difficulty in persuading such a person and if you did, I'm sure that they would expect to share in the possible reward you might receive. No, I have a better solution – Raul can accompany you. He is very streetwise and is authorized to carry a firearm. Won't that solve your problem?'

'Yes, and I must say that it's very kind of you to provide me with an escort.'

Zamarco tried to smile again. 'Right, then if you tell us where you are staying and what time you wish to go, Raul will pick you up and take you to Señor Gallardo's home.'

Mac tried to look embarrassed. 'I'm staying at the Hotel Rosario. It's only a two star hotel, but it's all I can afford at the moment.'

There was a low snigger from Raul and Zamarco said, 'Then if you do get a well justified reward from Señor Gallardo, you will be able to move to a better hotel.'

'Yes, but I'd rather spend the money on taking tours to places of historical interest.'

'So, what time should Raul call for you?'

'I'll be waiting in the reception area at seven, this evening, if that is okay.'

Zamarco looked knowingly at Raul, who nodded. 'Well, that's all fixed then, Mister Smurthwaite. Have no fear, Raul has Gallardo's address and will take good care of you.' Zamarco rose from his chair and extended his right hand. Mac stood up and gave Zamarco a limp shake of his sweaty hand.

'Goodbye and enjoy the rest of your holiday,' Zamarco said as Raul led Mac to the lift.

Mac caught a taxi back to the Hilton. Crossing the reception hall he noticed Sarah and Harry in conversation with Hank and joined them.

'What are you lot conspiring about now?' he said with a low laugh.

'I was just introducing Harry to Hank. They were very interested in each other's work. From what they were talking about one would think they had it in mind to exchange jobs, if that were ever possible,' Sarah said. 'Have you had a successful day, Mac?'

'Yes, I think I have and I might have some useful info for you later, Hank.'

'Good, I'll look forward to that.'

'Come on you two, let's have a quick lunch and then go and update Lionel on what's afoot.'

After a hurried and almost silent meal   Mac had said that most careless talk was carried out in restaurants   they took the lift to Durrance's suite.

Madge let them in and they found that Lionel was taking a nap on the balcony. Madge shook his shoulder until he awoke.

'You have guests, boss, and I'm sure they have lots to tell you.'

Durrance rubbed his eyes and sat up. 'Join me out here. As Clark Gable might have said, "I'm all ears to hear your news".'

Mac told them of his interview with Zamarco and the arrangement he had made with him to be picked up at the Rosario Hotel by his henchman, Raul.

'I can understand why you gave him a false name, but was it necessary to say that you were staying in that low class hotel?'

'Yes, very necessary, Lionel, because I wanted to give him the impression that I was just a poor simple soul, who wanted to do the right thing by returning the wallet and hoping that I might receive a reward for its return. I have a gut feeling that Zamarco is a very nasty piece of work who is a member of a drug cartel and uses his club as a centre for drug distribution.'

'So what if it is? How does that information help in any way to rescue our people?'

'The information would be very useful to the CIA and I've developed a sort of quid pro quo arrangement with them. We have received valuable help from them and I'm hoping that the information I may glean tonight will be worth a return favour. What you have to understand, Lionel, is that we need all the allies we can get on this mission and up to now we've not had any real help from the police and military authorities.'

Durrance ran his long thin fingers through his thatch of grey hair. 'I'm sorry Mac, you and Sarah come too well recommended by high sources for me to question your methods. I just hope that all goes well for you this evening, because our time is fast running out and I'm not receiving the financial support I'd hoped for from other film companies.'

'The reason for that is clear to me, Lionel,' Franklin interposed. 'It's that you have the filming rights to a fantastic story that will make a blockbuster of a film and your competitors are envious and would, I'm sure, hope that you will have to abandon the project and sell the screening rights. I've seen Mac in action and have every faith that he and Sarah, with a little help from me, will get our people back and finish the film in Brazil. Your main worry is Harvey Rheingold. He needs gingering up and you're the only man to do it!'

Durrance's pale face reddened slightly. 'If and when Harvey gets back to us, I shall deal with that. The last thing we want when making a film is to have the leading man and his director at loggerheads.'

*   *   *

Mac arrived by taxi at the Rosario Hotel at a few minutes before seven. Entering the hotel he sat in a chair in the foyer, where he would be seen by anyone entering the hotel.

At exactly seven o'clock Raul entered the hotel and walked over to Mac.

'I've a car waiting outside, Mister Smurthwaite. Have you got the wallet with you?'

'Of course,' said Mac, taking out of his jacket pocket and waving an old wallet, which he had stuffed full of telephone directory pages, cut to the size of Peso notes.

'Good. We can now leave for Gallardo's home,' Raul said, leading Mac out onto the street.

Raul stopped at the side of a large black saloon car. A man sat at the wheel. 'We'll sit in the back seats,' Raul said opening the door and motioning Mac to get in first.

When they were both seated Raul tapped the driver on the back and the car moved slowly away from the hotel to join the heavy evening traffic.

'How far is it to Gallardo's home?' Mac asked.

'Not very far, we should be there in ten or fifteen minutes,' Raul replied. 'But before we arrive, there is something I must do,' he said, producing an automatic pistol from his side pocket and pressing it against Mac's right temple. With his other hand he reached under Mac's jacket and withdrew Mac's pistol from its shoulder holster and placed it on the seat beside him.

'What the hell is this all about, Raul?'

'Why are you carrying a gun, Smurthwaite?'

'I brought it for extra protection.'

'Stop talking nonsense! You are a member of the US Drug Enforcement Agency, or if not that, then a CIA agent. Your weapon is fitted with a sound moderator and you are carrying it like a professional. And your name isn't Smurthwaite! I checked the Rosario Hotel and they confirmed that no one by that name was staying there.'

Still keeping his gun pressed against Mac's head, Raul took the wallet from Mac's pocket. 'As I thought, this was just a ruse to gain Gallardo's address,' he said shaking the paper from the wallet. 'You must have somehow gained information that Gallardo was one of our cocaine mules and wanted to get him to identify his employers.'

Mac laughed. 'You really are over the top, Raul. What you are saying is really nonsensical! Now put that gun away, give me mine and I'll not report your extraordinary behaviour to the police.'

'Shut up, Smurthwaite and enjoy your last ride!'

Mac looked out of the window and saw in the failing light that they were outside the city and heading into the countryside.

A few minutes later Raul tapped the driver on the back of the head. The driver drove to the side of the road and stopped the car against a grassed verge.

Looking out, Mac saw a wooden farm-like building set up in the middle of a field.

'Yes, you may well look at that building. It's one of our coca processing plants. You would have loved to have put it out of commission. Now it's to be the last thing you ever see. Get out of the car and stand on the verge,' he said as he picked up Mac's pistol from the car seat and pocketed his own weapon. 'It might be of some comfort to you that I'm going to shoot you with your own gun.'

Mac opened the door and stepped out of the car. Raul followed closely behind, his gun arm extended. Mac grabbed the door handle and slammed it back hard against Raul's arm. Raul screamed with pain and dropped Mac's gun. Mac scooped it up and before Raul could reach his own gun from the car seat, fired two shots into Raul's chest. Raul fell out of the car at Mac's feet. The driver reached into the dashboard for his gun and turned to fire over the seat at Mac. Mac fired a single shot into his forehead.

Mac checked the two bodies both were dead. He removed their wallets before rolling them into the ditch which ran alongside the verge. He unloaded their guns and threw the cartridges into the field and dropped the guns into the ditch. He didn't want children playing in the area to pick up loaded guns. Finding some cleaning rags in the boot he wiped the blood from the driver's seat, then got in, made a five-point turn and headed back to Bogotá.

On arriving back at the Hilton he was pleased to see that Hank was still on duty. 'We'd better use your office to talk. I've got some business for you,' he whispered.

Hank led him into the office. 'You look like you've had a very busy day Mac. Is that blood on your jacket?'

'Yes, but it's not mine!'

'What have you been doing to get bloodied?'

Mac related everything he had said and done that day.

'That was certainly a great bit of luck, you stumbling onto a coca processing plant. How far did you say it was from the city?'

'I was on the road north from the city and I checked the mileage. It was exactly twenty-three miles from the Hotel Rosario to the spot where Raul planned to terminate me. If you're planning to send some of your people out there to destroy the building you will find a couple of stiffs in the ditch opposite the building. It might be a good idea to put them in the coca building before you blow it up or burn it down. Oh, yes, and there's something else you might be able to do for me. I'm now the proud owner of a luxurious motor car, which is parked outside the hotel. It belonged to the late Raul and if his boss, Almondo Zamarco, alerts his troops to be on the lookout for it, new registration plates would make it more difficult for them.'

'No problem, Mac, I can rustle up some Panama plates and Bart can do the necessary and, I guess, remove any bloodstains from the interior of the car.'

'Thanks a million, Hank. Now, if you've got any handy, I'd like nothing better than a very large measure of Remy Martin, before I join my wife for a late dinner.'

When Mac entered his suite he was surprised to see Sarah, Durrance, Franklin and Madge seated around the dining table in deep discussion. They stopped talking when Mac approached.

'What, are you having a council of war?' Mac said with a laugh.

'Yes, I suppose we are doing something like that,' answered Durrance. 'We have much to tell you. But first tell us about your day.'

'I'd be more interested to hear what you are all excited

about. So, to get to the point, I found the El Fantastico Club to be a distribution centre for drugs. I've passed this info on to Hank, so I suspect it will soon be out of business. Now, what news do you have for me?'

'The bad news comes first,' Durrance said. 'This afternoon when Madge went to reception to collect the mail she was given a sealed hatbox. When we opened the box we were horrified to find Danny Bristow's head inside. There was also a note enclosed reminding us of the deadline to pay the ransom and details of the Bank of Panama account into which the money had to be paid. We took Danny's head to the Chief of Police and insisted that he get his men to make determined efforts to recover the hostages before it's too late. He promised to do all he could to rescue them.' Durance paused and took a sip of water. 'Better news is that we've heard from the British Consul that the Foreign Secretary has been bombarding the Colombian Government with diplomatic notes urging that the military and police authorities do all that is necessary to rescue our people. But the best news of all that we received today is that Omega Films have been authorized by the Brazilian Government to film in the area around Manaus, which as you know is a well-established city, near the Amazon River. They have also agreed that a whole floor of the Amazon Jungle Palace five-star Hotel will be allocated to our entire film cast and technicians while the film is being made and that the Brazilian Tourist Board will pay for the accommodation. Apparently, the reason for this is that because of the enormous public interest aroused by the exceptional media coverage regarding the film we are making, has resulted in a surge of holiday bookings by local and foreign tourists.'

'Well, that's certainly good news for Omega Films and tourist companies, but as you previously suggested, Lionel, it doesn't help us find your people. But what I have here might do just that.' Mac placed the two wallets he had taken from the dead gangsters. 'I'm hoping that these wallets contain documents and other papers that will lead us to where the hostages are being held. So, if you will excuse me and Sarah, we'll be off to get dinner followed by an early night in bed, where we will examine the contents of the wallets.'

Sarah took the hint and left the table. 'Goodnight everyone, we'll let you know in the morning if we've found anything useful in the wallets.'

CHAPTER TWELVE

26 MARCH

Although they had been awake into the small hours checking the papers in the wallets and planning what they should do in the morning, Mac and Sarah went down for an early breakfast. Returning to their suite they saw Hank standing at his desk dealing with a young couple. As soon as the couple walked away they approached the desk.

'Hi guys, you both look like I feel. I guess we should try to get to bed earlier.'

'So, you had a late night as well, Hank?'

'You bet, but it was very worthwhile. We torched that plant and got rid of a couple of million buck's worth of cocaine. It made a very fitting funeral pyre for those two drug pushers.'

'What about the El Fantastico Club?'

'Yes, it was visited. We beat the door down at 3 a.m. and the boss man and a couple of his thugs tried to stop us getting into the office, but got shot-up for their pains. We blew the wall safe and found a heap of US Dollars, Pesos and records giving details of where their next consignment of drugs was being shipped. As the club wasn't adjacent to any other building, we torched it before we left. All in all a real coup for our team and all thanks to you two. To do something to repay you, I've got a couple of my guys working undercover in the sort of places that baddies hang out and as soon as they come up with anything about your people, I'll let you know.'

'Thanks, Hank. I just hope I'll be hearing from you soon. We've only got five days left to rescue the hostages before those kill-crazy bastards start butchering the rest of the company.'

'I'll do whatever I can to get the info you need. But whatever the future brings, I have drafted a laudatory report of the help you have given the CIA, which will soon be on its way to our director. In the circumstances he may well decide to authorize me to take overt action to help you.'

'If you do come up with something, we'll be in our suite for the rest of the morning. After that I just don't know at present.'

Mac and Sarah didn't have to wait long. Hank rang them about two hours later. 'I have something for you, but don't want to pass it over the phone. I'll be up in a couple of minutes.'

Sarah let him in and they joined Mac around the dining table.

'It's good and bad news I have.'

'Let's hear the good news first, Hank,' Mac said.

'One of my agents, playing the part of a drug hooked local, was in one of those shady out of town clubs, where anything goes, when he heard a conversation between a couple of ugly customers that he and others were holding two of the female hostages in a remote suburb of the city.

The address was mentioned and my man made a note of it and rang it through to me. I have it here,' he said passing a piece of paper to Mac.

Mac read the address and passed the paper to Sarah. 'See if you can locate the place on our road map. Well, that's certainly good news, Hank, but let's hear what the bad news is.'

'Yes, I'm afraid it is very bad news. The rest of the conversation that my man heard was that the thug who passed the address to his companion was inviting him to his place to hire one of the girls for sexual pleasures. From what he said, it seems that this particular man has been making a regular practice of offering these two unfortunate women for hire since they were first kidnapped. The women have tried to resist the attentions of the men who have hired them, but this, he said, arouses the men to greater lust.'

'We can't let this continue, Mac, we must rescue those two women without delay. If you remember, Harry Franklin said that Moretta, the kidnappers' leader, promised that the hostages would come to no harm if Lionel Durrance followed his instructions. He seems to have lost control of some of his men.'

'Yes, and I hope the treatment the women are getting is not some sort of revenge, like the beheading of Danny Bristow, because of what we have done.'

Sarah shook her head. 'No, I shouldn't think so, because as far as we know he has no idea that we are in any way involved.'

'So, it's boots and saddles for you two. I'd love to join you in eliminating those scumbags, but if the director got to hear about it I'd be booted out of the CIA and lose my pension, or at least be reprimanded and downgraded.'

'No, I don't expect you to give us overt support. You've done enough. We can handle the rest.'

'Boots and saddles?' Sarah said with a puzzled look. 'I've never ridden a horse!'

'It's okay,' Mac laughed. 'Hank, Sarah's not familiar with some of your American expressions, but she's learning fast.'

'That's all right, I'm not too au fait with some of your British and her Yiddish expressions. But I've heard all about you and Sarah from the friends at the British Embassy, but you're still only two and you don't know how many of them you'll be up against.'

'From what we know, Hank, is that they seem to operate a system of two guards to each hostage. That allows them to maintain a twenty-four hours watch over their prisoners.'

'Yeah, that may be so, but you might find there's a queue of eager lustful customers waiting to take their turn with the women.'

'I take your point, Hank, but we will have the advantage of surprise and if Durrance will allow it, we can enlist the aid of Harry Franklin, who is a real gung-ho ex-infantry platoon commander, battle hardened in the first Iraq war.'

'He sounds as though he could be a useful recruit. But

I must get back to my desk now or I'll have a crowd of unhappy tourists complaining to my manager. Good luck to you both on your mission and I look forward to hearing from you how it all went.'

'Thanks again for your help, Hank and cheerio for now.'

As soon as Hank left Mac and Sarah tooled up (an expression Mac used when he was arming to go on an operation) and went next door to see Durrance. They found him in deep conversation with Franklin and Madge.

They all listened, appalled as Mac told them what Hank's man had heard about the two women hostages. 'I don't know who they were talking about. There were four women hostages taken, weren't there?'

'Yes, Gloria Duprez, Carol Farley, Ruby Benson and Clara Purvis. It's my guess and hope that Gloria and Carol have not been subject to their abuse. I'd better get on to the police. Give me the address, Mac.'

'Aren't you forgetting something, Lionel? The last time the police went to rescue two of the hostages, they shot them dead!'

Durrance wrung his hands in anguish. 'Well, what do you propose we should do?'

'You do nothing, but sit here and pray that Sarah and I can get those two girls back before they come to any more harm. And, if you're willing and Harry is prepared to join us, his extra gun would be a big help.'

'I'd be happy to join you, Mac, and get back at those swine. They'd get no quarter from me for what they are doing to those two girls, Mac.'

'I'm not happy about that, Harry; the President of Omega films has asked that you move to Manaus to receive the rest of the cast and technicians and be available to view the area where the filming is to take place and recruit some local extras.'

'To hell with what the president wants! I'm going to help Mac and Sarah to rescue those girls. I feel it is my responsibility to do just that!'

'Bravo, Harry, you're doing the right thing. Good luck to you all,' Madge said, clapping her hands.'

'What can I say, but good luck to you and get back safely,' Durrance said.

'Well, if we're going anywhere we'd better get going now. Have you got your pistol and extra ammo, Harry?'

'I certainly have, and am raring to get into action.'

'Then let's go!' Mac said, leading the way to the door.

When they reached the reception, Hank beckoned them to his desk. 'Your car is renumbered, cleaned and parked at the right-hand side of the hotel. Good luck!'

They found the car and Mac memorized the registered number.

'You sit in the rear, Harry, and watch out for any vehicle that may seem to be following us. Sarah, you be navigator with your road map marked with the kidnappers' address.'

Mac put the car into gear and drove away from the hotel.

'Navigator, can you give me an ETA at the speed I'm now driving?'

Sarah looked at the car's speedometer and checked the map. 'I'd say a little less than an hour.'

'Harry, when we get there, no gunplay from you, leave that to us. Our weapons have sound moderators on – that's because I don't want to alert the whole gang and any of their clients before we've got control of the place. We could be facing up to about half a dozen kidnappers, plus one or two visitors. When we go into the house, cover your face with your scarf. Remember you were seen by the kidnappers and if any of them survive and get away to tell Moretta, he'll know you are actively involved in trying to rescue the hostages.'

'Roger, Chief!' Harry replied with a laugh.

Mac drove the rest of the way in silence, only broken by Sarah's directions.

When they arrived at their destination it was nearly midday and the sun was high and scorchingly hot. Mac stopped the car on the other side of the road. Without getting out of the car they viewed the large detached house, which was surrounded by a six-foot high wall and overhanging trees. A large people-carrier was parked on the road.

'Why are we waiting here, Mac?'

'Because it's lunch time and it's my guess there's not much cooking being done in there. So, it's quite likely that one or two of their number will shortly be sent to some take-away shop to buy food. Should that happen we'll follow their vehicle and grab the guy as he stops at a take-away shop. We'll then persuade him to tell us who's in the house and what's going on there. He'll either have a key to the house or the gang will expect him to knock on the door when he returns. In either case the doorman will be silenced. We will have put two of them down and made an unchallenged access to the house. Of course, there's another possible scenario; a visitor might arrive by car for sexual gratification. We would hijack him and get him to knock on the door and deal with him and the doorman in the same way. Are there any questions?' Mac said with a short laugh.

'Not, from me Chief it's obvious you've done this sort of thing before.'

'He certainly has,' Sarah interposed.

Mac's hunch paid off. Ten minutes later a man came out of the house carrying a large holdall. He got into the people carrier and drove off. Mac immediately followed keeping a ten-yards distance behind the vehicle. A few minutes later a few shops and cafés came into view and the man slowed down to look out for the one he wanted.

'This is how we'll play it when he stops I'll get out of the car with you, Harry, and grab him. I'll keep him company in the back and you drive the vehicle in the direction from where we came and stop about twenty yards before the house. Sarah, you follow in the car.'

The vehicle stopped and the driver opened the door. Mac pulled in behind the vehicle and he and Harry leapt out of the car. As the driver stepped onto the pavement Mac rammed his pistol into the man's stomach. 'Get the back door unlocked,' Mac said in a quiet but menacing tone. The man looked down at the gun pressed into his belly and quickly produced a key for the rear door. Harry climbed into the driver's seat and waited for Mac's instruction to move off. Mac opened the door and pushed the man onto the seat and followed, keeping his pistol pressed into the man's side; he patted him all over to check for weapons.

'Right, away we go,' he called to Harry.

Harry made a five-point turn in the road followed by Sarah and both vehicles sped off in the direction of the kidnappers' house.

A few people witnessed what had happened, but took no notice. They were used to seeing people being dragged off the streets and being taken away in police or military vehicles.

'This'll do, Harry,' Mac said as they passed a wooded area with no buildings nearby.

Harry stopped the vehicle and Sarah drove in behind.

'Mabala usted inglesi?' Mac said, pushing his pistol into the man's stomach. The man paused, then said, 'Si, si, I speak good English.'

'What is your name?'

'My name is Alvaro. Why do you treat me so?'

Mac ignored his question. 'Have you a key to your house?'

'No.'

'How do you get into the house?'

'I press the doorbell and my amigo opens the door.'

'How many amigos are in the house?'

'Why should I tell you?'

'Because if you don't I shall put a hole in your head!'

'There are three men at the house.'

'I believe that there are two women hostages in the house,' Mac said as he pressed his pistol against Alvaro's temple.

'Yes, yes, señor, that is so,' Alvaro said in a tremulous voice.

'I have been told that you have been abusing these women.'

'No, not I señor, that was our leader and his amigos. They pay him money to fuck the women.'

'What is your leader's name?'

'It is Aurello.'

'Are there any of Aurello's amigos in the house?'

'There were none there when I left.'

'Now, up to now you've been very co-operative. If you remain so when we get to the house, I shall let you live. Do you understand?'

'Yes, yes, I shall do as you say, señor. Let God be my witness to that.'

'Okay, Harry, time to go. When we get there you stay with the vehicle, ready to drive off as soon as Sarah and I leave the house with the hostages. We'll put them in with you; then we'll follow you.'

Harry drove to the house and stopped at the kerb in front of the house.

'Pick your bag up, Alvaro. Get out and walk in front of me up the steps and ring the doorbell.'

Sandra joined them at the foot of the steps.

'Keep out of sight until I've dealt with the doorman, Sarah.'

Sarah positioned herself at the side of the door. Alvaro pressed the doorbell. A few seconds passed and the door was opened. The man uttered a few words in an angry tone. Then he saw Mac behind Alvaro and pulled a pistol from his belt and took aim at Mac. There was the muffled sound of a gunshot as Mac's pistol put a hole in the centre of the man's temple. Alvaro turned with a knife in his hand to strike Mac. There was another sound of a muffled gunshot, this time from Sarah's pistol, and Alvaro fell down the steps with a hole in the side of his head.

'Didn't you search that one for weapons, Mac?'

'Yes, for guns, but that one had a knife up his sleeve. It was a good thing I had you covering me.'

Mac entered the passage and pulled the doorman's body against the wall.

'That's two down and two to go,' whispered Mac. They both listened for a few seconds, but there was no sound coming from the downstairs rooms. 'They must both be upstairs with the women,' Sarah whispered.

They crept noiselessly up the stairs and stood on the landing. There was a noise of anguished cries from one of the rooms. Sarah quietly opened the door. As she did so there was the noise of a toilet being flushed and a man came out of the bathroom. Before he could utter a sound, Mac fired two shots into his chest.

As Sarah entered the room a man, naked from the waist down, got off the bed cursing and reached under a pillow for his gun. Sarah aimed her first shot low, very low. She was on target and the man screamed as he lost his manhood. Sarah paused while the man let out gut-wrenching screams until she silenced him with a bullet to his brain.

Sarah went to the naked woman on the bed. 'It's all over now. We're here to rescue you. Who are you?'

The woman sat up on the bed and pulled a sheet around her. 'Clara Purvis,' she replied in a tremulous voice. 'My friend Ruby is next door.'

Mac entered the room. 'I've seen Ruby; she was expecting unwelcome attention from the man who came out of the bathroom.'

'Are they all dead?' Clara said.

'Yes, every one of them; you're quite safe now. Harry Franklin is outside in a people carrier waiting to take you back to the city.'

'Do you want to have a quick clean-up in the bathroom?' Sarah said.

'No, I just want to get out of this awful place and have a long hot bath and get into some clean clothes. We've been wearing the same clothes since we were kidnapped.'

'I feel the same way,' Ruby said as she entered the room fully clothed.

'Take them to Harry and tell him to wait until I've searched this place for information about the location of the other hostages. You stay with the girls and while Harry is waiting for me he can get that body on the steps moved into the house.'

Mac searched the bodies and removed their wallets and

any papers he found. Next he searched every room in the house and removed any documents and papers, including Clara's and Ruby's passports, which he found in a desk drawer in the sitting room. He put all the documents and papers he had removed into Alvaro's holdall, shut the front door and joined Sarah and Harry.

'I see you managed to get Alvaro's body into the house, Harry.'

'Yes, he was only lightweight. Where are we going now?'

'We'll go to the hotel, for the girls to get cleaned up and into some clean clothes, which Madge can buy in the hotel shopping mall, then get them a meal. When that's been done I shall ring Hugo to send a car to take you and the girls to the embassy, to stay there until they fix you up with a new passport. You will then be able to take the girls to Manaus to link up with the people Omega Films are sending there.'

'I agree that you've got it all figured out right, Mac, but I'd sooner stay here to help you and Sarah recover the rest of our people.'

'Yes, we'd be glad to have you with us, but you've got a film to direct and Lionel would never agree to you being in harm's way any longer. That's our job. Now let's get back to the hotel. You, Sarah and the girls, into the people carrier and I'll follow in the car.'

*   *   *

As soon as Ruby and Clara had bathed, dressed in their new clothes and eaten, Harry took them to see Durrance, while Mac phoned Hugo.

Durrance was delighted to see them, and to note that they seemed relatively unscathed by their ordeal. They left the suite to be taken by Sarah to watch television until the arrival of Hugo's man later that evening.

Harry remained with Durrance and related the part that Mac and Sarah had played in carrying out their rescue.

'Your account of the incident has the makings of a thrilling film,' Durrance said.

'You're sure right about that, boss, and Mac and Sarah would be the best people to play the leading roles. In that film and the one we're making now. They're the best double act I've seen since Bogart and Bacall!'

'Are you suggesting that our two leading stars are not performing as well as I had hoped?'

'Well, to be honest boss, I don't rate Harvey Rheingold as an action man type. It's true he is handsome and has a good body, but that's as far as it goes. I think he'll be more acceptable playing the role of a male prostitute, like Richard Gere played in *American Gigolo*. Gloria is a good actress, but she doesn't convey the persona of a tough cookie. Anyway, neither of them will be playing any part if they are not found in the next few days.'

'We mustn't forget that Moretta said that for every member of our company who was killed or rescued the ransom money of the remainder would be increased. So, it is very unlikely that he will ever kill Harvey or Gloria.

It is my guess that he wouldn't bother too much if we rescued the other hostages and he might even decide to do away with them now and up the ante on our top stars. So, we aren't in such a bad state as we first thought. The minor stars and technicians wouldn't be too difficult to replace. And you haven't taken much footage so far and what you have done could be scrapped if we are going to film in Brazil.'

Franklin's eyes blazed with anger. 'Are you suggesting that we abandon the search for the others? Because, if you are, you can find yourself another director! I'd not work for anyone with such abominable disloyalty to his employees!'

Durrance leaned forward and patted Franklin on his arm. 'Now, now, Harry, don't get yourself all worked up. I was simply examining our options. We've been associates far too long to fall out at this stage; especially when we have such a major project to handle. Of course, it is said that no one is indispensable, so, if for any reason you want to leave my employ, I'd not stand in your way.'

'Point taken, Lionel, but to get back to the film, do you agree with Murphy's suggestion that I take Clara and Ruby to Manaus to await the arrival of the rest of the cast and technicians?'

'Yes, Harry, you go ahead as soon as you can. And while you're waiting, you can be looking for suitable filming sites along the Amazon.'

Durrance reached into his desk drawer and took out a bottle of 15-year-old malt whisky and two glasses and poured two generous measures.

'Now, isn't it better for us to sit here enjoying one of life's pleasures rather than engaging in a bickering match?'

Franklin nodded and smiled wryly as he sipped his drink.

Five generous measures later, there was a knock on the door. Madge was out with Sarah and her two charges. So, Durrance, too drunk or too lazy to answer the door, shouted, 'Come in!'

Mac entered with Sarah. 'Hugo's here to take you to the embassy with the girls. Are you ready to leave, Harry?'

'Yes, I'm all packed up and my cases are being held in reception,' Harry replied in a slightly slurred voice.

'Goodbye, Harry. Don't forget to keep me informed of what's happening in Brazil,' Durrance said with a slurred voice, as Harry followed Mac to the door.

'Sure thing, boss,' Harry called over his shoulder as he left the room.

Mac led the way to reception and Harry picked up his suitcases.

'That wasn't too smart of you two getting pissed at a time like this, Harry,' Mac said.

'Perhaps not, but we were settling some differences. And alcohol has always been Lionel's way of dealing with personnel problems.'

'Personnel problems   what's all that about?'

'Not now, Mac, I'll tell you some other time.'

Hugo was standing by an embassy limousine, talking to Sarah, as they approached.

Harry joined Clara and Ruby in the car and a porter put his cases in the boot.

'Thanks for all you two have done and I'm sure you'll do your best to rescue the others,' Harry said through the open window.

'Don't worry, Harry, we will! You just make your film, which we hope will be a real blockbuster!'

'I'll be seeing you, Mac,' Hugo said as he got in the car and drove off.

*   *   *

Mac and Sarah spent the most of the early evening searching through all the wallets and papers Mac had collected from the kidnappers' house; few of the papers, however, were written in English.

'I think we'll have to ask Hank to do the honours, Sarah. I'm sure some of these papers contain information useful to both the CIA and us. I'll give him a buzz and see if I can take this stuff down to him this evening.'

Mac rang Hank, who said he was taking a night off and would be glad to come up to their suite and go through the papers with them and translate as necessary. Five minutes later he was knocking at their door and entered carrying a bottle of Remy Martin and a bottle of Bollinger Champagne chilled to the right temperature.

'I know Remy Martin is your favourite tipple, Mac, but I suspect Sarah favours Champagne cocktails.'

'You're right on both counts, you clever little CIA

agent,' Sarah said with a laugh as she took the appropriate glasses from a display cabinet.

'We didn't expect this when you said you'd come up here to help us search through this lot,' Mac said as he opened the bottle of cognac.

'Ah, but you never know, we might have cause to celebrate if we find some useful intelligence in these papers.' Hank expertly opened the Champagne bottle.

Mac spread all the papers and documents out on the dining table.

Hank picked out all driving licences and personal documents, which he said might come in useful for his team. Next, he scanned through all the papers, notes and diaries and set some aside for further study. When he had seen all the material he went back to those he had set aside and studied them carefully, making translated notes in a slim notebook he produced from his pocket.

'Bingo!' Hank said, excitedly waving a small diary. 'We've hit the jackpot!'

'Well, what is it that you've found that's so exciting?' Mac said.

'This diary belonged to a man named Aurello Bedoya, one of Moretta's lieutenants.'

'Yes, Sarah had a brief meeting with him. He'd been raping two of the film technicians. Sarah put him out of business in no uncertain manner…'

'Never mind that, this is extremely important,' Hank interrupted. 'According to the notes in this diary, Bedoya had instructions from Moretta to rendezvous with his men tomorrow at a town called Condo. I've heard about the place – it's in the Antioquia province, not too far from the coast. Years ago it was little more than a small village, home to a few farmers and their families. Today, it's a cocaine boom town crawling with drug traffickers. The police patrol the area armed with assault rifles, but they are not very effective in dealing with the heavily armed groups that roam in the region.' Hank paused to take a swig of cognac.

'Why would the kidnappers go all that way? They are not in that league of drug vendors,' Mac said.

'No, but a shipment of US small arms is being delivered there from a source in Panama. Moretta must be recruiting more men and will need to arm them.'

'I can see why you are so interested about this information, Hank, but what about the hostages? They surely wouldn't have planned to take them with them.'

'No, they wouldn't. According to what's written in the diary, Moretta ordered that they be killed before Bedoya and his men left for Condo. So, as it happened, you saved them before Bedoya carried out his orders. I have to say, Mac, you always seem to do what you have to do at the right time.'

'Yeah, it comes with practise, Hank. But what's your next move?'

'I shall take a few days furlough and go to Condo to attempt to destroy that shipment of arms or turn it over to the military authorities. I shall also destroy any stockpiles of cocaine I locate.'

'Do you think there's any chance the kidnappers are holding any of the hostages in that town?'

'Hmm...it's 250 miles from Bogotá, so it's unlikely, but Moretta and some of his men must be there to get the arms shipment. And he might be thinking of using some of the high-priced hostages to pay for the weapons. In fact, that may have been his intention when he kidnapped them. Hostages are seen as a sort of currency by several of the insurgent groups.'

'Two-hundred and fifty miles, that's a hell of a way by car! You'd need to travel tonight or at first light tomorrow to get there before Moretta gets the weapons and leaves.'

Hank laughed softly. 'That's no problem. We have the use of a helicopter and can be there in about two hours. I would return tomorrow evening.'

'I know what you're thinking, Mac, before you say it,' Sarah said. 'You want to go with Hank, hoping that some of the hostages are being held there.'

'Well, it did cross my mind Sarah, but we've only got four days left to find them and the chances are that they are more likely being held in or near Bogotá.'

'I understand that the hostages must be your first priority, but if you do want to come with me, I'd be glad to have you aboard; and no matter what my director says, I'll do everything I can to help you find the remainder of the hostages.'

'Okay, I accept your offer, Hank.'

'I'd like to go too, but one of us must stay and follow up on any leads that may come to light,' Sarah said.

'Yes, but don't you try to go it alone,' Mac said. 'You just go through all those documents again and see if anything gives a clue as to where any of them are being held.'

'We'll take off at 06.00 hours, so be down at reception at 05.00 hours. Bart is driving us to our landing strip. Four of my section members will be there waiting.'

'Who'll be flying your chopper, Hank?'

'One of my two former Air America pilots will be at the controls and the other one will be on board as a back-up if the pilot becomes a casualty.'

'That's very comforting to know, Hank. Your agency is certainly well organized and leaves little to chance.'

'Yes, we've learnt a lot from previous foul-ups, which have cost us dearly.'

'If you guys are getting up so early, don't you think you should go to bed now?' Sarah said as she corked the bottle that contained what little was left of the Remy Martin.

'You're right, Sarah, I'll now take my leave and see you in the morning, Mac. Goodnight to you both.'

Before going to bed Mac checked their two Glock automatic pistols and fully loaded the magazines. He laid out a fresh set of jungle clothing and put two spare magazines and the sound moderators into the bush jacket pockets.

'I've left that pistol that Harry had to leave behind in your bedside locker. If things go as we've planned I shall be back tomorrow evening. If any problems arise that you feel you are unable to deal with, phone Hugo.'

'Yes, darling, now let's have a shower before we go to bed.'

Thinking of what could happen to him next day, it occurred to him that it might be the last shower he shared with Sarah. 'That's something I've looked forward to all day,' he said.

CHAPTER THIRTEEN

27 MARCH

Bart was standing by his car when Mac and Hank came out of the hotel. They got into the car and sat on the back seats. They both had matters they wished to discuss before they reached the air strip.

'Are you ready to go, boss?' Bart called over his shoulder.

'Yes, Bart, and don't spare the horses,' Hank called back.

'I appreciate you coming along, Mac. You know how to handle yourself and I hope the trip is going to be worthwhile for you. But I don't want you to take any wild chances. I'd hate to have to report you as a casualty to my director and your ambassador.'

'It'll all be worthwhile if I can get any information about the hostages. So I'll be on the lookout for Moretta or any of his men to help me with my inquiries.'

'That sounds like the term your police force use when they have a suspect in custody.'

'Yes, it is, Hank, but my inquiries can be a lot more persuasive than those of the police. My suspects don't get cups of tea and cigarettes, but I usually get the information I want from them.'

'And there was me thinking you Brits were against torture.'

'We are, Hank, but there are times when it is necessary to adopt more persuasive measures when you're dealing with some of the lowlife types that refuse to tell you what you need to know.'

'We're here, boss,' Bart called over his shoulder.

Mac and Hank got out of the car and walked to where the helicopter was parked. Four of Hank's men were standing near it and as they approached one of them came to meet them.

'Everything we might need is loaded and the aircraft is ready for take-off, Chief.'

'That's fine, Steve.' Then, moving to the other men, he said: 'This is Mac Murphy you've all heard about him. He's coming with us on this mission, so treat him like one of us.'

The men murmured their assent and shook hands with Mac as they boarded the helicopter.

Hank sat up front with the pilot and Mac took his place with the other men.

There was little conversation during the flight. Mac thought that in spite of their chief's introduction, the CIA agents were still a little unsure as to how much Mac knew, or should know, about their present mission.

Hank and the pilot exchanged words about their present position and where they should land.

Mac wondered how far the landing site would be from Condo and how they would travel from there to the town with all the equipment they were carrying.

A little under two hours and the pilot started to descend. Mac looked out and saw that the pilot was going to land on a small clearing next to a heavily wooded area. As the helicopter landed a black Chrysler Grand Voyager drove out from the trees and stopped a few yards from the helicopter.

'All out!' Hank called out.

His men got out and stood around the helicopter waiting for his instructions to board the Voyager.

The driver of the vehicle, a tall, husky, rugged-featured man in his forties, looked the sort of man with whom you wouldn't want to pick a fight. He approached Hank and gave him a mock military salute. 'You made good time, chief.'

'Yes, Carlos, we did, and I'm glad to see you arrived on time to meet us. You can unload the baggage hatch and get the equipment stowed into your vehicle.

Carlos unlocked the baggage hatch and started to remove the equipment. Hank's men helped him carry the equipment to the car and he loaded it.

While this was being done Mac joined Hank. 'I was wondering what transport you had up your sleeve to get us into Condo. I see it has seating for seven men. Is that a fortunate coincidence that we are seven, or was it forward planning?'

Hank gave a little laugh. 'In CIA we always ensure we have the appropriate equipment to do the job.'

'Your Carlos looks a pretty useful sort of guy. Is he a CIA agent?'

'No, like Bart, he is one of my locally recruited men. I know what you're thinking, Mac   can he be trusted? He certainly can. I've had every detail of his pedigree checked out. I do that with everyone we employ or anyone with whom we have any sort of dealings.'

'So, you've had me and Sarah checked out?'

'Yes, and liked what we found out about you and your wife. A couple of independent and real-life James Bondish type operatives, who, as far as the US security services are concerned, always do your stuff on the right side of the fence.'

'What do you want me to do while you're blowing up illegal arms shipments and cocaine warehouses, Hank?'

'You stay with us and if we turn up any of the kidnappers we'll give you any support you might need to deal with them.'

'I probably feel the same way as you do about drug trafficking and gun–running, so I'd be more than happy to help you with your intended purpose.'

'That's great, Mac. Stay by me; I couldn't wish for a better right-hand man!'

The loading completed, Hank told everyone to get into the Voyager.

'Are you going to leave the chopper unguarded, Hank?'

'Yes, it should be okay here, Mac. Very few vehicles ever pass this little more than a dirt-track road, and if government troops found it they'd identify it as a CIA aircraft and would see no harm came to it. As to any insurgent groups who might come across it, there's no way it could be guarded with less than a platoon of Special Forces men. In the unlikely event that the aircraft is damaged or destroyed we'll return to Bogotá in this vehicle.'

'What mileage can you get out of this vehicle?'

Hank paused in thought. 'Oh, about 30 mpg, I'd guess.'

'So, apart from what you use driving in Condo, you'll need about eight gallons of fuel to get us back to Bogotá.'

'Yes, Mac, you're about spot on with your calculations. I'll check with Carlos to see what we have on board.'

Hank called Carlos over. 'What fuel is in the tank and in reserve jerricans?'

'About four gallons, chief.'

'That's not enough to get us back to Bogotá.'

'No, but I thought you'd be using the chopper to get back.'

'Yes, we probably will do just that, but there's always a chance that when we return to the aircraft we'll find that it's been sabotaged by insurgents. So, at the first opportunity I'd like you to get another five or six gallons.'

'Okay, chief, I'll see to that. But if you drive the Voyager back to Bogotá, how do I get home?'

'We'd drop you off at your home before we went back to the city. Anyway, let's roll now. I want to be on the road outside Cumbal within the hour because, if my information is correct, that's where the gun-runners will turn off to go to Condo.' He turned and looked at the others.

'All aboard!' he ordered.

'Well, I must say, Hank, you certainly run a tight ship and your intelligence sources seem pretty reliable,' Mac said as he climbed into the Voyager.

Carlos drove off and kept within the speed limit.

'How far is it to Cumbal?' Mac said.

Hank, who was sitting next to Carlos, turned to face Mac. 'We'll be there within fifteen minutes.'

'What's the drill when we get there, Hank? Are you going to arrange some sort of ambush?'

'Yes, something like that. What usually happens is that the lorry carrying the weapons has an escort car in front. We deploy a couple of men to cover the lorry and two others further back to signal when the escort vehicle comes into sight. If the occupants of the car intervene when we attack the lorry, we'll know they are part of the gang and take them out before they can get away.'

'Where do you want me when the action starts, Hank?'

'Just stay with me. We can keep back a few yards, to take on the escort car if it passes through our first line of defence.'

'This is the spot, chief,' Carlos said and braked the vehicle.

The four CIA agents leapt out of the Voyager carrying their weapons, which Mac identified as Colt XM177E2 Commandos. It was a most practical weapon, being shorter and lighter than the M16 assault rifle. It was much favoured by US and worldwide security units and Special Forces because it was easily concealed.

The four agents positioned themselves as Hank had planned.

'Carlos, stay with the Voyager and pull over under those trees, but be ready for an instant take-off as soon as we all return to the vehicle,' Hank ordered, as he and Mac got out of the vehicle and made their way back down the road about a hundred yards, where they positioned themselves behind bushes at the side of the road.

'I'm sorry we didn't have spare Commando rifle for you, Mac. What have you got with you?'

'A pair of 9mm Glocks,' Mac said, pulling the two pistols out from under his bush jacket. 'These have more hitting power than those 5.56 mm rifles you and your men are using.'

'Yes, but they're fitted with thirty round magazines, so we can loose off a barrage of gun fire at our targets. The rifles are also fitted with M203 grenade launchers.'

'That's a high waste of ammo. It only takes one bullet to put a man down, so...'

What Mac said was lost in the sound of two explosions and a fusillade of gunfire.

'They've hit the lorry and here comes the escort vehicle,' Hank said as he levelled his weapon in readiness to fire. He fired a burst at the car as it came alongside their position. The bullets bounced off the vehicle.

'It's an armoured vehicle!' shouted Mac, as he fired at the tyres.

The tyres burst and the vehicle skidded into bushes at the other side of the road. Four men carrying assault rifles got out and attempted to take cover behind the car. Hank emptied his rifle at one man who was still exposed. As he was reloading two of the men came out of cover to take advantage of Hank's vulnerability. Mac stood up with a pistol in each hand and took careful aim at the two men who were about to fire at Hank. A bullet from each of his guns hit both men in the head. They both fell dead in a heap on the road. The fourth man threw down his weapon and raised his hands above his head.

'Get out from behind that car and come over here!' Mac ordered.

The man walked slowly towards Mac with his hands raised. Still covering him with a pistol, Mac patted him down for hidden weapons. There were none.

'Remove all documents and wallets from those bodies and bring them to me. Then roll the bodies into the ditch,' Mac ordered.

The man complied without a word. He was terrified and wanted to live. He handed Mac the three wallets and a bunch of papers, which Mac stuffed into his bush jacket pocket.

'So you do take prisoners, Mac,' Hank said.

'Yes, I'm not normally into cold-blooded killing and there's always a chance that this one may have some information I want.'

Hank's men joined him at the roadside. 'We knocked out the lorry and the crew, Chief, but most of the cases of weapons are still intact,' the man named Steve said. 'We've also got a casualty. Tyler took a stray bullet in his shoulder.'

'Was he a victim of friendly fire?' Mac muttered.

There was no response to his question, which confirmed to Mac that it was.

'Steve, torch the lorry and their car. And you, Barney, render first aid to Tyler,' Hank said authoritatively.

Carlos got out of the Voyager and joined Hank and the others. 'If we're taking that man back with us, it's going to be a bit cramped in the vehicle.'

'Well, he's your prisoner, Mac – are you going have him sitting on your lap?' Hank said, grinning wryly.

'I'd like a quiet word with you, Hank,' Mac said, leading him a few yards away from the others and the prisoner who was still standing with his hands on his head.

'I just want ten minutes with this man. If he tells me what I want to know I'll leave him here alive. You could then phone through to your army contacts to have him picked up.'

'Okay, Mac, but no more than ten minutes. We can't hang around here too long. There may be insurgent groups waiting for their weapons to be delivered and decide to see what's causing the delay.'

'Then I suggest you and your men get ready to move off as soon as I've finished with the prisoner. He understands English, so I'll be able to communicate with him.'

Suddenly, there were two enormous bangs as the petrol tanks of the gun-runners' vehicles exploded.

'Right, see you in the Voyager in ten minutes, Mac.'

As soon as Hank and his men were in their vehicle Mac turned to the prisoner. 'Put your hands down and tell me your name.'

The man licked his lips nervously. 'My name is Pancho. I am a good man. I have a family. Please be merciful to me.'

'If you want to live you must tell me all you know about the British hostages who were kidnapped by Moretta. If you refuse to tell me, or lie to me, I shall shoot you in the head.'

'Señor, I know all about the kidnappings. My leader said that Rafael, he is Moretta's number-one man, was to pay for the weapons with two of the hostages. He said that they were worth two million US Dollars each, which the film company would pay us.'

'Where and when are the hostages to be handed over to your leader?'

'They are being held in the Hotel Andrada in Condo and we were to collect them this evening, when we delivered the arms.'

Mac pressed his pistol against Pancho's temple. 'Have you told me all that you know about the kidnapping and the deal to exchange weapons for the hostages?'

'Si, si, señor, on my mother's life I have spoken the truth. Please have mercy on me. I have a wife and three children.' Pancho trembled with fear.

'Good, I'll let you live to look after your family. There's just one thing I want you to do before I leave you. Throw those weapons into the burning car.'

Mac remained covering Pancho as he picked up the rifles and threw them into the blazing car.

'Adios, Pancho,' Mac said as he walked to the Voyager.

As he climbed into the vehicle the bullets in the gun magazines started to explode in the heat of the blazing car.

'Did you get the information you were after, Mac?'

Hank asked as Mac settled into his seat and removed the wallets from his pocket.

'Yes, two hostages are being held by Moretta's men in the Hotel Andrada in Condo. I need to be there this evening for the hostages for weapons exchange. Here's a bonus for your men to share,' Mac said, handing the wallets to Hank.

'I'll join you, Mac. Your visit to the Hotel Andrada promises to be an exciting action. But I think you should have silenced that man. He might get a message through to Moretta.'

'No, he's had quite a fright being so near death that it's my bet that Pancho will part company with his guerrilla comrades and go home to look after his family.'

'By the way, Mac, I guess I owe you my life for your quick draw on those two that had me cold in their sights. Wherever did you learn to fire two guns at once with single-handed holds?'

Mac gave a little laugh. 'I suppose it was all those old western films I saw as a boy, when only women held a gun with two hands. Clint Eastwood fired two guns from his hips and never missed a shot. Another thing is that when you use two hands to hold the gun facing your enemy, you make a nice wide target for him. But if you stand sideways to face your opponent, holding your weapon in one hand, you become a much narrower target.'

'That seems to make a lot of sense; I must try it next time I get involved in a gunfight.'

'Another gunfighter trick is to always have your last round in the breech before you reload.'

'How do you know when you've only got one round left?'

'Simple, just count the rounds you fire. Then, when you cease firing to insert another magazine, your adversary will expose himself, because he thinks he's facing a defenceless opponent, but you nail him with that last round you've got in the breech.'

'Any time you want to change your job, Mac, I'd be happy to recommend you as a small arms instructor at our training school.'

'Not on your Nellie, mate,' Mac said with a laugh. 'I've had my fill of being in a disciplined service. I prefer to be a freelance agent.'

'I can understand that, Mac, but who the hell is Nellie?'

'Who knows and who cares? More importantly, were you serious about helping me to take on the kidnappers?'

'Yes, of course I was, Mac. It's the very least I can do after what you did for me today.'

'Pancho didn't know how many of the kidnappers would be at the Hotel Andrada. As there are only two hostages with them, my guess is that there's not likely to be more than four or five. They'll have a truck with them to carry away the arms.'

'I'm reluctant to involve any of my men, Mac, and I want to get Tyler to our clinic to have his wound treated. So, I suggest that Carlos takes my men back to the helicopter and Tyler and the rest of my men are flown back to Bogotá. Steve can radio Bart to be at the airport to meet them and then take Tyler to our clinic.'

'That sounds like the right thing to do, Hank, but what about the Hotel Andrada?'

'As neither of us is known to the kidnappers we can go to the hotel and book in for the night and then do a recce of the place to find out where the hostages are being held and what sort of opposition we have to face.'

'That sounds fine to me, Hank.'

'Carlos, when we reach the Hotel Andrada, drop me and Mac off. Then drive Steve and the other guys back to the helicopter. When you've done that come back to the hotel, but don't enter the hotel. Stay parked outside, ready for a quick getaway when we come out. How far away are we now?'

'About three miles, Chief.'

'You're not going into the hotel with that weapon of yours, are you, Hank?'

'I have a slicker with me that should cover it.'

'There are three things wrong with that, Hank. You won't look right wearing a raincoat in this heat and certainly not in a hotel. If you have to bring your weapon into play it could get tangled up in your coat. But worst of all it can't be silenced. And we can't afford to be blazing away. The noise of gunfire could bring in more of Moretta's henchmen. I'll lend you one of my Glocks and a spare magazine. That'll give you over thirty rounds, which even for you should be enough ammo.'

'Thanks, Mac, I accept your offer. I have received training in the use of that weapon.'

'We're here, Chief,' Carlos said as he applied the Voyager's brakes.

Mac quickly pulled out one of his pistols, a sound moderator and a spare magazine and handed them to Hank, who put them away in his jacket pockets.

'As soon as we get out, drive away, Carlos,' Hank said.

Mac and Hank quickly got out of the vehicle and walked into the three-storeyed hotel advertised as "Three Star".

Mac surveyed the reception area and thought, the hotel wasn't awarded three stars for cleanliness. The floor was littered with cigarette butts, scraps of food and spilt drinks. A scruffy young man sat on a sagging armchair smoking an obnoxious smelling cigarette. An AK 47 assault rifle rested against the side of the chair. An equally untidy middle-aged man stood behind the reception desk and eyed them suspiciously as they approached the counter.

'We'd like to book in for one night, please,' Mac said.

'Do you want a double room with a double bed,' the man said with a suggestive leer.

'No, we want separate rooms.' Mac said.

The man checked his register. 'I only have one double room available for a one-night stay.'

'Okay, we'll take that if it has two single beds.'

The man sighed deeply. 'I will arrange for the beds to be changed. Will you complete these forms and let me see your passports?'

Mac leaned across the counter. 'Unfortunately, our passports are with our wives and they are staying in Bogotá. We're only here for one night and return to Bogotá tomorrow. Can you make an exception to your normal rules?' Mac almost whispered, as he slid a fifty-dollar bill across counter.

The man licked his lips and covered the bill with a large horny hand. 'Yes, señor, but you must complete these booking forms.'

Mac nodded and took the two forms and passed one to Hank. They completed the forms, using fictitious names and addresses, and passed them back to the man.

'I have no one to help with your baggage. You are in Room 3 on the second floor,' the man said, handing Mac a key.

'That's quite all right, we're travelling light,' Hank said with a wide grin.

They were followed by the young man with the AK47 rifle as they went into the lift. Mac pressed the button for the second floor. They got out on the second floor, but the young man remained in the lift.

As soon as they entered their room, Mac drew his pistol, fitted its sound moderator and placed the gun under a cushion on the sofa on which he was sitting.

Hank looked a little puzzled by Mac's actions. 'What's that all about, Mac?'

'I'm just taking a simple precaution, Hank. The man who followed us into the lift and got out on the third floor looks to me to be one of Moretta's men. It's my guess he was sitting in reception for two reasons. He was waiting for the arrival of the arms shipment and to check on who was entering the hotel and report their presence to whomsoever is in charge on the third floor. The fact that we had no baggage and were only booked for the night makes us very suspicious. He noted we spoke in English, so he thinks we are Americans and possibly CIA agents, here to deal with the gun runners. That being the case, we may get a visit from a couple of the kidnappers.'

Hank was convinced by Mac's precautions and took out his pistol and fitted the sound moderator. There was only one armchair in the room, so he sat on the end of one of the single beds and placed the gun under a pillow, then lay back on the bed with his right hand under the pillow.

'Shouldn't we be scouting around upstairs to find out where the hostages are being held, Mac?'

'No, let's wait and see if we get a visit. If we do, we must make sure we leave one of our visitors alive. We can then persuade him to take us to where the hostages are being held.'

Suddenly, there was the sound of whispering coming through the door.

'It's our visitors. Stay on the bed but don't produce your gun until I come into the room and then follow my action,' Mac whispered as he quickly and quietly went into the bathroom and left the door slightly ajar.

The door opened and two men entered the room.

'What is the meaning of this intrusion?' Hank said in a pompous tone.

'We're the hotel security officers,' said one of the men.

'That doesn't give you the right to enter my room in this manner. I shall report your unseemly behaviour to the hotel manager.'

Both men guffawed loudly. 'The manager sent us here to speak to you. He suspects that you are in possession of narcotic substances, which are not permitted in this hotel,' the spokesman said.

'That's very strange, because when we arrived there was a young man in the reception smoking an awful smelling home-made cigarette. I'm sure it was one of those banned narcotic substances.'

'Never mind that, we want to know what you are doing here?' the spokesman said.

'We're tourists; here to take in the local scene.'

'Where's the other guy that you came in with?'

'I'm here,' Mac said as he emerged from the bathroom with his pistol levelled at the men.

The men reacted instantly. Their hands dived under their coats to withdraw their guns.

Hank fired two shots through his pillow at the leading man's chest. The man dropped dead at the foot of the bed. Mac fired at the second man's gun arm. He screamed with pain and dropped his gun.

The wounded man fell back into the armchair whimpering.

Mac pointed his pistol at the man's head. 'Now, if you don't want to finish up like the man on the floor, I want you to answer a couple of simple questions. Where are the hostages?'

'What hostages, I don't know anything about hostages.'

Mac pressed his pistol against the man's forehead. 'I can see I'm wasting my time, so I'm going to finish you off!'

'Okay, okay   please don't kill me. They're on the top floor in room 23.'

'How many more like you are there with them?'

The man hesitated. Mac pressed his pistol between the man's eyes.

'There are three others. One man is with the hostages and two are in room 25.'

'Are they all armed with AK 47's?'

'No, only Paulo has one. The others have automatic pistols.'

'Is Paulo the man we saw in reception?'

'Yes, he was there to await the arrival of a truck.'

'Which room is Paulo in?'

'He will be with our leader, in room 25.'

'Is Rafael your leader?'

The man looked surprised. 'Yes.'

'Get up; we're now going to take you for a little walk to see if you've been telling us the truth.'

The man stood up nursing his wounded arm. Hank frisked him for weapons and removed his wallet from his hip pocket. He went through the dead man's clothing and removed his wallet. He removed the magazines from the two pistols and put them in the lavatory cistern.

'Right Mac, I think we're ready to go.'

'Yes, we are. You lead the way to room 23,' Mac said opening the door and pushing the man into the passage. The man went to the lift and Mac opened the door and pushed him into the lift. He and Hank entered and Mac pressed the button to take them to the third floor. The man led them to room 23. Mac opened the door and using the man as a shield pushed him into the room. With his pistol drawn, he quickly surveyed the room. Two bound men were sitting on a sofa. Their guard was sitting in an armchair toying with a cell phone. An automatic pistol was on a side table. The guard, seeing Mac and Hank behind his fellow kidnapper, went for the pistol. He had it in his hand when Mac's single shot hit him in the head. With the top of his head blown away there was no need to check his life signs.

Hank untied the hostages and handed one of them the dead man's pistol. 'Don't make a sound. The rest of the gang is next door.'

Hank opened the door to room 25 and they entered, their pistols drawn, their prisoner in front. They were met by a burst of fire from the man with the AK 47. As their prisoner, hit by a half a dozen bullets, dropped to the floor, they returned fire. Paulo, who was in front of Rafael, took three bullets in his chest and two in his head. As he fell he exposed Rafael, who fired wildly, shooting lumps of wood from the door jamb and nicking Hank in his upper left arm. Mac and Hank both fired at Rafael's chest and he staggered back and fell to the floor. Mac checked the three bodies and was not surprised to learn that they were all quite dead.

'How bad is that wound, Hank?' Mac said as he saw blood oozing through Hank's jacket sleeve.

'It's not life-threatening; it's just a flesh wound.'

Mac helped Hank take off his jacket and ripped his shirt sleeve to look at the wound. 'It's not serious, but I'll put a tourniquet on to stop you bleeding to death.'

Mac ripped Hank's shirt sleeve into two lengths and joined them, then tied it tightly around his upper arm.

'That should do until we can get you to a hospital. Now let's see how the hostages are.'

When they entered room 23 the man whom Hank had given the gun stood pointing it at them.

'Okay, guys, you're safe now. You can put the gun away,' Mac said. 'What are your names?'

The man with the gun said, 'I'm Paul Landers.'

'I'm Barry Robbins and I'm very pleased to see you,' said the other man. 'But you're not police officers, are you?'

'No, my name is Mac Murphy and I've been commissioned by Lionel Durrance to rescue you. My co-rescuer is Hank, a member of the CIA – without his help I couldn't have carried out your rescue. You'll note by the blood on his jacket that he's been wounded so we haven't got time for conversation because I want to get him to a hospital for treatment.'

'There's no need for hospital treatment, Mac. Carlos can take me to our tame doctor who is on our payroll. But we don't want to hang around here anyway. We might get a visit from the hotel manager, who must have heard the gunfire and if he sees all these bodies, he'll call the police. Because of the help we're giving them in dealing with the drug cartels, the CIA does have an amicable relationship with the police, but I don't want to have to explain to them and my director about my involvement in non-CIA operations. So, let's hit the road – speaking of which, I hope Carlos is back.'

They took the lift down to the reception and went to the door.

'Hey, you guys haven't paid your bills!' the receptionist shouted.

Mac went to the counter and tossed about five hundred US dollars onto the counter. 'Here, that should more than cover the total bill and I've added some extra cash for your cleaning staff.'

As soon as they got out on the street, Carlos saw them and drove up to the hotel. Hank got in the Voyager and sat beside Carlos. Mac sat with the two actors on a bench seat behind. Carlos drove off at speed.

'Where do you want to go now, chief, the clinic?' Carlos said, noticing the bloodstains on Hank's jacket.

'No, take these people to the Hilton first, and then I'll direct you to where I want to go.'

'I do want to get Paul and Barry to the Hilton as soon as I can, but we ought to get your wound attended to first,' Mac said, genuinely concerned for Hank.

'No, it won't take longer than four hours to get you there and my doctor isn't very far from the hotel; but there is something you can do for me on the way. Stop at a clothing shop and get me a jacket and shirt. After I've seen the doctor, I don't want to turn up at the hotel wearing this bloody jacket and torn shirt. I'm a 42 regular.'

'Okay, Hank, but there is a shopping mall in the hotel, which seems to be open all hours, so when we get there I'll get what you need there and bring it out to the car.'

'Good thinking, Mac, I'd forgotten about that facility.'

'We'll soon have you guys reunited with your producer. I imagine your first priority is a hot shower followed by a substantial meal,' Mac said.

'Yes, you're right there. Can you tell us what has happened to the other members of our group?' Paul said.

'I'd like to leave all that until we get back to the hotel. We'll want all the information you have about your kidnappers and Lionel should be present for the debriefing session.'

'Will Harry Franklin be there, Mister Murphy?' Barry asked.

'No, he's gone to Manaus to meet up with the other members of your cast coming from the UK. Lionel has arranged for the film to be finished in Brazil. No doubt he'll arrange for you to go there to join the others. By the way, I don't suppose you still have your passports?'

'No, they were taken from us when we were first kidnapped,' Paul said.

'That's no problem; Madge can take you to the British Embassy sometime to have replacements issued.'

'We're here in record time!' Carlos said, slamming on the brakes at the entrance to the hotel.

Mac looked at his watch. It was almost ten o'clock.

'You two come with me and stay in the reception area while I get Hank's duds. As soon as I've done that I'll take you up to join Lionel.'

Mac went straight to the clothiers and bought a lightweight tan jacket and shirt and took them out to the car. He passed them through the car window to Carlos.

'Keep them away from Hank until his wound has been properly bandaged.'

'Thanks, Mac. By the way here's your Glock, a very useful weapon,' Hank said, pulling it out of his belt and handing it to Mac.'

Mac went back into the hotel and beckoned Landers and Robbins to join him at the lift.

'We're now going to meet your producer, who is a very anxious man and will want to question you at length. I imagine you'll feel more inclined to that after you've had a shower and a proper meal. We'll get room service to bring up the choice of today.' Mac tapped on Durrance's door and it was answered by Madge.

Madge wrapped her arms around Mac's neck and kissed him on the cheek. 'I'm so pleased you're back safely and with two of the cast. Come in, Lionel will be delighted to get some good news. He's been like a cat on a hot tin roof all day.'

Madge led them out on to the balcony. Durrance was stretched out on a sun lounger, drinking whisky. A near empty bottle of malt whisky occupied the side table.

'Look who's here! It's Mac and he's rescued Paul and Barry.'

Durrance tried to get off the lounger and stand up, but failed, so settled for a sitting position.

'Thank God you're safe! Sit down and tell me all about everything that's happened to you.'

Paul and Barry were about to do that, but Mac intervened. 'Hold your horses, Lionel. These guys have had a pretty rough time. So, give them a break to get cleaned up and fed.'

'I'll get room service to bring up meals for them and Mac while Paul and Barry get showered, and then fix them up with some robes to wear until we can get some new clothes for them,' Madge said.

'Oh, very well, but we can talk while they are eating,' Durrance said a little testily.

'I haven't seen Sarah since I returned and I'd like her to be in on the debriefing. So, I'll pop next door for my shower and change of clothes and bring her in,' Mac said.

'Yes, of course, Mac,' Durrance said in a slightly slurred voice. 'We owe you and Sarah so much for what you've already achieved and it looks like you are now our only hope in getting the rest of our people back.'

Mac let himself in. 'Your loving husband is here, darling, and he wants a homecoming kiss, a shave, a shower, a change of clothes and a large Remy Martin.'

Sarah came into the sitting room from the balcony and walked into Mac's open arms. He embraced her and they kissed passionately.

'Yes, you certainly need a shave and a shower,' Sarah said with a laugh and held her nose. 'I'll join you in the shower when you've had a shave.'

Mac quickly shed his clothes and went into the bathroom. Sarah poured drinks and placed the glasses on the sofa table. She then stripped off her clothes and put on a bathrobe. She opened the bathroom door and called, 'Are you ready for me?'

'I certainly am,' Mac replied opening the door of the steam-filled shower cubicle.

Showered, shaved, clothed and sipping Cognac with Sarah on the sofa, he quickly related what had happened at Condo. 'We managed to bring back two of Lionel's actors. They are with Lionel and Madge getting cleaned up and having their first decent meal for days. Lionel's very anxious about holding a debriefing session and he wasn't very far from being the worse for wear with whisky when I left him. I suppose we'd better go in and find out if there have been any developments while I was away. Have you anything to tell me?'

'I went through the rest of those papers you salvaged and there are some addresses we ought to investigate, but that can wait until we've had our session with Lionel.'

Mac tapped on Lionel's door and Madge let them in. 'Wowee, Mac, it's amazing what a shower, a shave and sex can do for a man's appearance! We're all waiting to hear your account of how you managed to free Paul and Barry.'

Madge led them out onto the balcony, where Lionel was in deep conversation with the two actors. They both stood up when Mac and Sarah entered and Lionel wrestled himself into an upright position. Mac noticed that the whisky bottle was gone.

'Paul and Barry have been telling us all about the way you dealt with the kidnappers. That's the good news,' Durrance said.

'What's the bad news, Lionel?'

'I've received another message from Moretta. He says

that if I want my two top stars back, it'll cost me twenty-five million pounds! And if we don't pay up before the first of April, we'll get the heads of the other four hostages back in boxes!'

'That's what he has said all along,' Mac said with an edge to his voice. 'Every time a hostage is rescued or killed, the ransom of those remaining is increased. So, let's put his threats aside for the moment and talk about what we are going to do about rescuing the four people who are in immediate danger.'

'Those four are Carol Farley, Rick Morales, a couple of untried supporting actors; Bruce Dawlish, a cameraman and Omar Rashid, a not very experienced security guard. All of whom…'

'I know what you're thinking, Lionel,' Mac interrupted, 'that they're all expendable and easily replaced! We don't have to worry about your top actors. They're Moretta's final bargaining chips. He'll see that no harm comes to them. If you never raise the ransom money one of the big studios will step in and pay the ransom, which will obligate your two stars to move over to the studio that has bought their release.'

'If that should happen we'd probably still have to pay off Rheingold and Duprez what they are contracted to get and we'd have to find two other stars to replace them!' Durrance said in a quavering tone.

'I don't profess to know how you do business in the film world, Lionel, but if your two top stars walked out on their contract, surely you'd be off the hook.'

'That might be so, but we'd end up facing a lawsuit which could cost us millions and a lot of bad publicity.'

'Okay, let's put all that aside and think positively about our next moves. Firstly, I suggest you arrange for Paul and Barry to get replacement passports and for them to join the other members of your party in Manaus. Sarah has obtained some addresses of the possible whereabouts of the other hostages, which we'll check out this evening. I should think that Moretta has personally taken Rheingold and Duprez out of the country, possibly to Panama, where his bank is located and from where he could conveniently travel by road, sea or air, to anywhere in the Americas.'

'Well, Mac, you seem to be on the top of your game, so I'll leave you to do what you know best. Madge will deal with the administrative matters tomorrow morning,' Durrance said with a slight return to sobriety and composure.

'Well, we'll be off now, Lionel, to study the info that Sarah's got and then to see how Hank is. With regard to Hank, the concierge, his involvement in the rescue mission and any future assistance we might get from him or any of his men, is strictly confidential and not to be mentioned to anyone outside our immediate circle. If what he's been doing for us got to the ears of his director or the media he might find himself out of a job or even facing prosecution.'

'I quite understand, Mac, and I'll ensure that nothing is said by our people to jeopardize his undercover activities.'

'I'm glad to hear that, Lionel. Now if you'll excuse us, Sarah and I have to get back to checking out the kidnappers' likely bolt-holes.'

Back in their suite, Sarah gathered together the documents and papers which had been taken from the kidnappers and started to look for addresses.

'Never mind that now, Sarah, let's see how Hank is. Bring the papers with you; he might be able to help.'

Hank was at his desk when they entered the reception area. As soon as he saw them he opened his office and beckoned them to join him.

'How's the arm, Hank?'

'It's okay. Our doctor soon put it right. He said the dressings will come off in a couple of days and assured me there will be no lasting ill effects to my arm.'

'That's good news, Hank.'

'Yeah, but I've had some bad news. My director has got wind of my wounding. His main concern is that my cover might have been blown and he'll have to recall me to Langley.'

'How the hell did he find out about that, Hank? I don't believe it came from Durrance or any of his people.'

'I don't really have a clue! It could have been from our doctor; a member of my section, who might want to discredit me in the hope it would put him in the frame for promotion; or it could even have been Moretta, whose spies are everywhere. Anyway, I told him that because of the way you had helped us, I considered it was only right that I should repay the debt. After all we do have a special relationship with the United Kingdom and are usually on the same side. However, while he has expressed his appreciation of your past help, he has given me clear instructions not to engage in any further operational missions with you, without his personal authority.'

'That's a pity, Hank, because I was going to ask you to give us some help to check out some locations where it might be possible the kidnappers are hiding out.'

Hank threw back his head and laughed. 'Of course I'll help you, Mac. In my book, checking out addresses is not a CIA operational task; it's a basic administrative job!'

'I couldn't agree more, Hank, and I much appreciate your offer of help. Give him the papers, Sarah, and we'll go and see if our MI6 friend in the British Embassy has any news for us.'

'MI6? I thought your spooks were now called the Secret Intelligence Service (SIS).'

Mac nodded. 'Yes, that's right, but old titles die hard and both are used by the old hands at the game.'

'I'll get on with checking out these addresses and try to get some answers for you by tomorrow morning.'

'Thanks a million, Hank. If you do have any useful info and we're out, please have it passed under sealed cover to Durrance's PA, Madge Burton.'

'I'll see that is done, Mac. Good luck to you both in whatever you're next planning to do.'

'Thanks and cheerio for now,' Mac said as Hank followed them out of his office.

Outside the office there was a group of guests who

were waiting to have restaurant and theatre bookings made for them.

Back to the day job, thought Hank, as he put on a broad smile and said: 'Good evening folks, what can I do for you?'

CHAPTER FOURTEEN

29 MARCH

'What's our plan for today, Mac?' Sarah asked as she stepped out of the shower stall.

'That all depends on what Hank comes up with. But we'll need to give him a little time to check out any addresses he finds in the papers you gave him. We can fill that time with contacting our embassy friend to see what he and others have managed to find out about the kidnappers and their abductees.'

'You mean Hugo Bickerstaff?'

'None other, darling. But remember, the "friends" don't like their names bandied about outside the embassy,' Mac replied as he dried his feet.

'I know all about that. We had similar unwritten rules in Mossad.'

'Sarah, as soon as we're dressed we'll order a room-service breakfast. Then I'll give Hugo a ring and see if I can persuade him to come to lunch with us. We'll take him to some out-of-the way restaurant where he won't be known and we'll have some privacy to talk. I know he is usually fish-eyed and rather dour, so I'm hoping you will use your feminine wiles to get him to open up with anything he, the ambassador or the Foreign Secretary's department, have managed to find out from the Colombian authorities.'

'Feminine wiles, indeed! I'll not let him think me some sort of femme fatale trying to loosen his tongue. But I will try a little gentle persuasion and exercise some of my Mossad-trained techniques in questioning unresponsive suspects.'

'I'm sure you'll have more success than me with those techniques,' Mac retorted, flicking his bath towel across Sarah's rear.

Breakfast over, Mac rang the British Embassy and after some delay was put through to Hugo. 'Are you free for lunch today, Hugo?'

There was a short pause before Hugo replied: 'That depends on who's paying for it.'

'We will, of course. I know how poorly paid you not-so-public servants are.'

Another pause. 'Where have you got in mind?'

'We'll leave that to you. I realize you won't want to go anywhere you might be known. So pick a secluded place that's some way from the city centre and provides excellent cuisine.'

'Hmm…there is a place that's been recommended to me by a French diplomat who takes his current mistress there. He says the staff members at the restaurant are very discreet.'

'Good, that sounds like what we want. What's the name of the place and how far is it from the Hilton?'

'La Escudero, and it's about a fifteen-minute drive from your hotel. Your taxi driver will know the way.'

'Is 13.00 hours okay for you, Hugo?'

'Yes, that's the time I usually go for lunch, but we call it one p.m. in the Diplomatic Corps'

'Right, we'll get there at that time. My Spanish is worse than my Japanese, so would you book a corner table for three? Use any name but ours.'

'Mac, you're making me work for my lunch!' Hugo said with a rare laugh. 'I'll book the table in the name of "Algernon Arbuckle" and the tab will be down to you.'

'I have to say it, Hugo, being humorous is not your thing. We'll be at La Escudero sharp at 13.00 hours.'

Mac rang Hank and asked him if he could have the services of Carlos to take them to La Escudero.

'Yes, that'll be okay, I'll brief him to pick you up from here at 12.40. He knows the restaurant and has taken me there several times. I can recommend the food. Oh, yes, I might have something for you later today.'

'Thanks, Hank, I hope it provides us with a lead.'

Mac and Sarah went down to reception at 12.30 and sat near the entrance. They saw Carlos pull up in front of the hotel at exactly 12.39. He's given us a minute to get into the car and then we're off that's precise timing, thought Mac. They walked out of the hotel and got into the car. Carlos set off without a word. Mac looked at his watch as Carlos pulled up at the restaurant. It was 12.55. Hank certainly keeps his men on the ball, he thought.

'Just give me a ring on your cell phone when you're ready to return to the hotel, boss, and I'll be here in a couple of minutes,' said Carlos.

As they got out of the car, they saw Hugo getting out of a taxi. They waited at the door until he joined them.

'You made it here on time, Mac. You were lucky. You must have had a good taxi driver. It sometimes takes three times what it ought to get anywhere in Bogotá.'

'Yes, we had a very good taxi driver,' answered Mac as he led the way into the restaurant.

A smarmy-faced *maître d'* looked up from his desk at Mac. 'Have you a reservation, señor? '

'Yes, we have, for three, in the name of "Arbuckle",' Mac replied, glowering at Hugo.

The *maître d'* looked down at his reservations list and nodded. 'Yes, you asked for a corner table.'

Mac nodded his reply and the *maître d'* beckoned an unoccupied waiter. 'Table 14, Anton.'

Anton led them to their table and handed them menus. 'Can I get you wine or cocktails?'

Mac looked at Hugo for his answer. Hugo shook his head. 'Water will do me. The ambassador doesn't approve of lunchtime drinking when we've got meetings in the afternoon.'

'What about you, Sarah?'

'Water is fine for me.'

'Still water will do, please,' Mac said to the waiter.

They gave their orders and the waiter filled their water glasses.

As soon as the waiter left their table, Hugo said, in a low voice, 'I am quite aware that there is no such thing as a free lunch, so what's this all about, Mac?'

'We've no sinister motive for inviting you to lunch, Hugo. We simply want to know if there have been any positive diplomatic efforts made to recover the surviving members of the Omega Film Company's personnel.'

'Yes, of course there have. The Foreign and Commonwealth Office ministers have been bombarding the ambassador with notes every day, wanting to know what progress is being made to recover the abductees.'

Mac grimaced. 'I know all about that diplomatic note exchanging bullshit, Hugo; what I want to know is what overtures are being made to the police and military authorities?'

'We're told that the matter is receiving constant attention. But the abduction of all manner of people is so prevalent that the authorities are unable to guarantee their release. The authorities say the only sure way to secure their release of abductees is to pay the ransom demanded.'

Before Mac could reply the waiter returned with their first course. As soon as the waiter was out of earshot Mac leant over the table to be closer to Hugo. 'Don't you have any underworld contacts and people on your books who'll sell information to you if the price is right?'

'Yes, I've a few people who provide useful information from time to time, but I've been instructed by my director and the ambassador that I must not get personally involved in this matter. He has heard reports, from the police and others, that you and Sarah have been actively involved in the rescue of some of the abductees and were possibly responsible for the death of some of Moretta's men. As far as I can gather, the police and military authorities are quite happy for someone like you to do their job for them. That's of course if they can claim some of the credit for your successes. However, the ambassador is in a very different position and is bound to follow the instructions of our foreign secretary. He has also been told not to permit any of his diplomats to give you anything more than limited support. I'm sure he would be most displeased if he knew I was having lunch with you, which may lead to compromising my position.'

'All right, Hugo, you've made your point; you've fed me a load of diplomatic claptrap. But I was once a soldier and see the matter differently. I took on the job after being persuaded by your Ralph Jermayn, who I understand was acting under the orders of the Foreign Secretary, to do all in our power to recover the abductees. So you can understand that we now have every right to feel that we've been cut adrift without covert support from your department. Some might liken it to a double-cross!'

'I'm really sorry you're taking such a negative view, Mac. I can tell you what you and Sarah have already achieved is highly regarded and I'm sure will not go unrewarded at some future date.'

Mac gave a short laugh. 'You mean we might appear on some sort of honours list as having been awarded putty medals for causing an international incident by rescuing a party of British subjects who had been abducted?'

Before Hugo could reply, Sarah, who had been engrossed in their conversation and had waited for the meal to be started, said: 'The soup's cold now.'

'Yes, it is,' said Mac beckoning to the waiter to fetch their main course, which they ate in virtual silence.

Hastily finishing his meal, Hugo looked at his watch.

'I'm afraid I can't join you for dessert, I need to be back at the embassy before two-thirty.'

'That's all right, Hugo, there's nothing more of value to discuss and, anyway, Sarah and I have a busy afternoon, so we'll forgo dessert.'

Sarah nodded agreement and Mac summoned the waiter for the bill.

Mac waited for Hugo to leave before ringing Carlos to come and collect them. He settled the bill and by the time Sarah had been to the rest room and they left the restaurant, they found Carlos waiting outside.

On arrival back at the hotel Mac thanked Carlos for his service and slipped a twenty-dollar bill into his top pocket.

As they passed the concierge's desk they saw that Hank was engaged with a group of guests.

They had barely time to take off their jackets before there was a tap on the door. Mac opened the door to see Madge standing in the passageway holding an envelope.

'I heard you return so I came straight away to give you this envelope. It was brought to me by the concierge. He said it wasn't to be opened by anyone other than you or Sarah.' Madge handed the envelope to Mac. 'Lionel wanted to know what it was. He became very annoyed because I wouldn't let him open it.'

'Thanks, Madge,' Mac winked. 'You did the right thing for all concerned. I'll pop in to see your boss later to smooth his ruffled feathers.'

'What have you got there, Mac?' Sarah asked as Mac sat on the sofa and opened the envelope.

'It's from Hank   addresses of Moretta's men, I hope.'

Mac spread the papers out over the sofa table and scanned them page by page. 'Ah…here's a likely hideaway a nightclub. Hank's marked it in red.'

'What's it called?' Sarah asked, her interest aroused.

'La Cucaracha Club.'

'I don't know much Spanish,' Sarah said, 'but I think a cucaracha is a cockroach.'

'You're right, and you can't get much more of a low-life than that, especially if it is in a restaurant,' Mac answered.

'That's a rather off-putting name for a club, where, no doubt, food is served.'

'No, not as surprising as it may seem, Sarah. It was, I once was told by a Mexican, the name of a Mexican revolutionary song. He told me the words in English, but we haven't the time for me to wrack my brain over such trivia. I'll bring it up some time when we've nothing better to do.'

'I take it then that we'll be making a call on this home for cockroaches?'

'Yes, my dear, as soon as we get dressed up like the locals who'd frequent such a dubious club.'

Mac and Sarah went shopping in a nearby crowded market place. They bought outfits of cheap clothing, as worn by lower-class locals. On the way back to the hotel, Sarah noticed that Mac was limping more than usual and obviously in some pain. 'What you need is a walking stick, Mac.'

'Yes, I do miss my old stick, which had more uses than simply making walking easier.'

'You mean your swordstick, which you couldn't take on the aircraft. I know they are illegal in the UK, but I should think you could get one here.'

'Yes, you're probably right. I'll ask Hank when we get back to the hotel.'

When they arrived back, they waited in the reception area while Hank dealt with a guest. As soon as he was free they went to his desk. Mac told him they liked his suggestion that the La Cucaracha Club was a likely place in which to find Moretta's henchmen.

'Watch yourself there. Mac, I've been asking around and the word is that the place is always full of desperadoes. Even the police avoid going there.'

'Thanks for the advice, Hank. I know you've been warned off giving me any active support in what I'm doing, but there is something you might be able to do for me.'

'What's that old buddy?'

'It's my gammy left leg. It's been playing up a bit lately.'

'You need a walking stick,' Hank interposed. 'You could have got one in that market you were in.'

'Yes, but I need one that can be used as a weapon.'

'You mean a swordstick? They are available, but off-hand I don't know of a shop that would sell them. But I'll ask Carlos. I'm sure he'll know where they can be bought. If he can get one I'll ask him to bring it here.' Hank called Carlos on his cell phone and spoke a few words in Spanish. 'Yes, he knows where he can get one and will bring it straight back here. I guess you want to have it with you when you go clubbing?' Hank said with a broad grin.

'Yes, I shall feel much more active with one. Thanks a lot, Hank, for your trouble. When Carlos gets here we'll be up in our suite getting changed into this local gear we bought.'

'Yes, you do right in exchanging your rather formal British attire for what the locals wear, especially when visiting the La Cucaracha Club. See you later.'

Mac and Sarah had hardly finished showering and changing into their new clothes when Carlos arrived with a swordstick wrapped in brown paper. Carlos tore off the wrapping and handed the weapon to Mac. 'There's a small button under the handle. You press that and a six-inch blade shoots out. To withdraw the blade, you hold the button down and press the blade against a firm surface, but nothing that will blunt the point. The shopkeeper did it against a piece of wood.'

'This is just what I want and I'm familiar with this type. How much do I owe you, Carlos?'

'Well, it's second-hand, but in good condition, so I didn't think that sixty-five bucks was too much to pay for it.'

'Second-hand or not, it'll suit my purpose. Here, take this and keep the change,' Mac said, thrusting a US 100-dollar bill into Carlos's hand.

'Thanks, boss. You're a great guy to do business with,' Carlos said as he left the suite.

Mac spent a few minutes practising releasing and withdrawing the blade.

'You're happy now you're armed with your favourite weapon. But what about firearms, are we taking them?'

'Yes, I think we'd better. I'll fit sound moderators to them. A spare magazine each should be enough. You could carry your pistol in that leather shoulder bag. Have it hanging at the height you can easily reach into if you have to use it. A shoulder holster and harness won't fit too well under this close-fitting jerkin, so I'll stick my pistol in my belt.'

'With all this weaponry, are you expecting that we'll be going into action – rather than simply visiting a dubious nightclub where the worst that might happen is that we'll be overcharged for our drinks?'

'Now, Sarah, after us having been engaged on some pretty hairy operations, hasn't it become apparent to you that I always expect the worst will happen and go prepared for instant action? It's what I've been trained to do.'

'Yes, I know, Mac, and I generally agree with your preparations and plans of action, but sometimes the carrying of firearms can, if detected, alert your adversaries to initiate the action. There is also the possibility that to prevent guns and knives being brought in, clubs or other houses of social activity might have metal detection devices fitted to their entrance doors. You must realize that my military training turned me into an effective female warrior, but I also had the advantage of Mossad training that imbued me with caution and the use of a psychological approach when going into any kind of action.'

'All right, my dear, you've made your point. So, to deal with that possibility, I suggest I carry both our pistols and you walk slightly ahead of me carrying a metal object in your bag. If you set off an alarm we can abort the mission and return later without the pistols. If we get through without setting off any alarms I'll slip one of the pistols into your shoulder bag. Are you happy with that arrangement?'

'Yes, darling. That should work. I have to admit that whatever problem arises you always come up with a solution.'

'Right, that's enough chat! Stick a few of those uncollected spoons and forks in your bag and let's get to work.'

Passing through the reception area they saw that Hank had a queue of guests at his desk and didn't make eye contact with them.

'Couldn't Carlos have driven us to the club, Mac?'

'Yes, but I don't want to take advantage of Hank's help. We'll catch a taxi a few yards away from the hotel.'

'Why not outside the hotel?'

'Because I don't want any of the doormen knowing our destination, Sarah. Remember, Moretta has spies everywhere!'

They walked around the block and stood on the edge of the pavement. After less than a minute a taxi drew up. 'La Cucaracha Club,' Mac said.

The driver nodded and they got into the taxi. The taxi took them down ill-lit streets to what must have been the meanest part of the city. The driver braked his taxi in front of the club, which garishly flashed "La Cucaracha" above its entrance. 'This is it,' the taxi driver muttered. 'You, Americanos, pay fifteen dollars.'

Mac didn't bother to correct the man's error, but thrust a twenty-dollar bill over the man's shoulder as they got out of the taxi.

As they approached the entrance a brutish-looking, thickset man, wearing an ill-fitting commissionaire's uniform, opened the outer door to admit them. He looked them over before opening the inner door. As they entered, Sarah leading the way, Mac was poised to react if an alarm bell sounded. None did, so he moved closer to Sarah and shielding her shoulder bag from view, slipped her pistol into the bag.

The club room was crowded and a quartet played loudly from a small stage at one end of the room. A flight of stairs led up to a passage-way, which encircled the upper floor.

A waiter approached them. 'Have you a reservation, señor?' the waiter asked in English. Mac shook his head and slipped a ten-dollar bill into the man's hand. 'We'd like a corner table near the door, please.'

The waiter smiled obsequiously and led them to a vacant table near the door. He quickly cleared the table of glasses and crockery. 'What will you have to drink?' The waiter asked, dropping a food and drink stained menu on the table.

Without looking at the menu Mac said: 'Two large cognacs. Remy Martin, if you stock it.'

The waiter nodded. 'Yes, we do have that brandy, but few customers ask for it because it's very expensive. They drink the local brandy.'

While they were waiting for their drinks, Mac surveyed the crowded room. When the waiter returned with the drinks he paid for them and added a twenty-five per cent tip. The waiter beamed. 'Mucho gracious, señor!'

'We are here to make contact with Señor Diego Contrero Moretta, or any of his men and we've been told they sometimes frequent this club,' Mac said in a low voice.

A look of fear came into the waiter's eyes. 'I have only seen Señor Moretta here once, many weeks ago. His men come and go now and then, but they don't mix with the other customers,' he almost whispered.

Mac slid a twenty-dollar bill on the table and said in a low voice: 'Are there any of his men here now?'

The waiter licked his lips and hungrily eyed the bill. 'There is one man here, who has been in company with Señor Moretta's men. He sits alone at the foot of the stairs to the upper floor.'

Mac looked across the room and saw a thin-faced, grey-haired man of about fifty drinking wine. A bottle stood on the table.

'Do you know what wine he is drinking?' Mac said as he slid the bill across the table to where the waiter was standing.

The waiter grabbed the bill and stuffed it into his apron pocket. 'Si, señor, it is a very cheap Chilean wine that many of our customers drink'

'What is the most expensive wine that you have in stock?'

The waiter screwed up his face in thought. 'We have few bottles of vintage Chateauneuf-du-Pape. It is not shown on the wine list, because it is only kept for our very wealthy and discerning customers.'

'What is your name?'

'Miguel, señor.'

'Right, Miguel, I'd like you to do me a small service. I want you to take a bottle of Chateauneuf-du-Pape across to that man and tell him who it is from.'

'What is your name to tell him, señor?'

'There's no need to do that, just point to our table. There will be another tip for you when I pay for the wine.'

After the waiter had left their table, Sarah said: 'You're being very generous   over-tipping and buying expensive wine for a stranger.'

'Never mind that, Sarah. It's only using a sprat to catch a mackerel,' Mac replied with a broad grin.

'There you go again, darling, with one of your odd expressions   talking about fishing, which has nothing to do with what you are doing.'

'That's where you are mistaken, my dear. I'm using small bait to catch, I hope, a big fish.'

They watched Miguel delivering the wine to the apparently surprised man and pointing across to them. Mac gave a wave to the man, who waved back and said something to Miguel. Miguel returned to their table and Mac paid him for the wine, adding a generous tip.

'Señor Arturo Baquero thanks you for your generosity and invites you to join him to share the wine with him.'

Mac gave Arturo a wave and they left their table to weave their way through the crowded tables. As they approached Arturo's table he rose and put out his hand, to which Mac responded and was surprised by the man's strong grip. Sarah put out her hand, expecting it to be shaken, but the man raised it to his lips and kissed it.

'I do hope you won't think us intrusive, but we're Martin and Sabrina McFee,' Mac said, coining false names. 'We're holidaying in your beautiful country. We don't know anyone here and seeing you sitting alone and not seeming to be part of this rather noisy and convivial scene, we thought you'd have no objection to us joining you to, perhaps, learn something about your country.'

Arturo beamed. 'Intrusive? Not at all! I'm always pleased to talk to visitors from other countries. From your accent I judge you to be English.'

'Yes, we are and must compliment you on your command of the language.'

'I noticed that you were having some difficulty in getting through the crowded floor, Mr McFee. And I see you have a walking stick. I don't mean to be impertinent, but you seem rather young to need one. Have you had an accident?'

'No, it's just an old war wound I suffered in Iraq. By the way, forget Mr McFee, I'm called Marty by everyone that knows me.'

'So, you were in that awful war that proved to be unnecessary and so costly in lives.'

'Yes, I agree, Arturo, it was a war that should never

have happened, but if you don't mind, I'd rather not dwell on the subject.'

'I quite understand, Marty, it was wrong of me to mention something that doesn't show Britain in a very favourable light. This is a great pity when one considers the enormous contribution Britain has made to the advancement of civilization.'

'Of course,' interposed Sarah, 'the Middle East is not the only place in the world that is suffering internal strife. I understand that you have serious problems here. Before we left to come here we were advised against all but essential travel to rural areas bordering Panama, Ecuador and Venezuela. We were also told that there is a high threat of terrorism in Colombia, which includes indiscriminate attacks, targeting government buildings, public transport, public spaces and other areas frequented by foreigners.'

'That's enough of that, Sabrina; you'll have Arturo wondering why we ever came here!'

Arturo gave a slight chuckle. 'Yes, I was beginning to think just that! However, I'm sure you both had a very good reason for spending a holiday in Colombia.'

Miguel came to the table with three wine glasses and opened the wine bottle.

'The wine is for Arturo, Miguel. We'll stay with Remy Martin. Fetch a bottle, please.'

Miguel returned with a bottle, opened it and filled their glasses. He was going to look after this group – the tips he was getting nearly amounted to what he was paid in a week.

Mac took a sip of brandy before he reopened the

conversation. 'With regards to what you said about why we had chosen to come to Colombia for a holiday, I have a confession to make, Arturo. The fact is we are a pair of free-lance journalists, who travel the world to report on unusual cases that have aroused interest throughout the world.'

Arturo's eyebrows rose and he looked intently at Mac. 'There are many unusual happenings in Colombia, Marty. What drew you here?'

'To cut a long story short, we had recently returned from an assignment and were looking forward to a short break before taking on another, when one of our left-leaning editors broke the story of the abduction of a group of film makers, who were being held for ransom by an anti-government insurgent named Diego Contrero Moretta. He promised us the earth if we could get an interview with this man. So, that is why we are here.'

'Aha…now I see why you try to cultivate me with expensive wine and affable conversation! You must have been told by Miguel that I have a connection with this man Moretta.'

Mac put on a contrite expression. 'I apologize, Arturo, I admit we were only trying to establish a connection with you that might lead us to locating Moretta and getting the interview.'

'Well, I don't know what Miguel has told you, but the relationship I had with Moretta has long been ended. He started out as a left-wing insurgent with ambitions to help the down-trodden under-classes to achieve a better standard of living. Sadly, his method of doing this led him to acts of terrorism against the government and the kidnapping of government officials, members of the military and police forces and, more recently, foreign tourists, to raise money to finance his activities. In short, he has become nothing more than a bandit, who seizes every opportunity to gain personal power and wealth.'

Sarah leaned over the table and gave Arturo a winning smile. 'I gather from what you say that Moretta did start out with the right intentions, that is, of course, if you consider the way to Communism is the right path to take a country. If that is so there may be a slight chance to encourage him to mend his ways and revert to his initial endeavours.'

Arturo smiled at Sarah. 'I'm afraid you are too hopeful, Sabrina, for such a change of heart on his part. He has long since burnt his bridges and when the military or police finally give their full attention to dealing with him he will become another casualty in the on-going war against the Communists and other anti-government insurgents.'

'Well, to be perfectly honest with you, Arturo, whatever he intended to do, or has done, will make a damn fine featured article for any newspaper, magazine or television documentary,' Mac snapped.

'That may be so Marty, but you will have to catch the bird before you can pluck it!'

'I'm well aware of that and was hoping that you might help us find him.'

Arturo shrugged his shoulders and grinned, displaying irregular, coffee stained teeth. 'And why should I help you find him, Marty?'

'Because if you do I'll make it well worth your while.'

Arturo's eyes widened and he sat upright in his chair. 'How much do you consider would make it worth my while?'

'How does ten thousand US dollars sound?'

Arturo gulped. 'That's a princely sum and it makes me wonder how much you expect to receive for your article.'

'That's not for you to concern yourself. I have been assured that I would receive a lot more than that for an exclusive interview with Moretta.'

'I can't guarantee that Moretta would risk attending an interview. He might think it was some sort of trap set by the police. Where would you conduct it?'

Mac refilled Sarah's glass and his own before he answered. 'I suggest on neutral ground. Are you married, Arturo?'

'No, my wife died ten years ago. Apart from my housekeeper, who works for me during the day, I live alone.'

'Then your home would be an ideal place to have the interview. Moretta does trust you, doesn't he?'

Arturo drained his glass and refilled it. Why not indulge myself, he thought, ten-thousand bucks buys a lot of wine.

'I haven't seen Moretta for about three years, but although we parted company because of his turn to banditry, I don't think he holds a grudge against me and if you met him under my roof it would go a long way to gaining his trust. But I feel sure that he'd expect some payment for the interview. Would you be willing to pay him a similar amount?'

'Yes, I would be happy to pay him the same amount. Now, what about contacting him? Have you any ideas as to his location at present?'

'No, I'd have to go through my old diaries to check for places where he might be. Failing that I might be able to contact one of his men. They do come in here quite often.'

'When you can come up with a likely location ring me, and I'll come to your place. You can then try to make contact with him. If you do I'll leave you to negotiate the arrangements and the amount of money he wants. Let me have your address and phone number; here's my phone number.' Mac passed a slip of paper to Arturo. Arturo scribbled out his address and phone number on a paper napkin and passed it to Mac.

'I think we should clinch the deal with a toast,' Sarah said as she refilled all the glasses.

'Right, I'll give you this to toast,' said Mac raising his glass, 'here's to our success in interviewing Señor Moretta, which should be of financial benefit to us all.'

They clinked glasses and swigged their drinks.

*　　*　　*

As soon as Mac and Sarah returned to the hotel they called

on Durrance. Mac gave him a very brief summary of what they planned to do.

'Who is this guy who is prepared to be so helpful?'

'There's no need for you to know that, Lionel. The fewer people that do the safer it will be for him. If he rumbled that he was being conned and Moretta found out he'd soon wind up dead.'

'Mac, I am beginning to wonder who's running this show. You're treating me as though you don't trust me. You should remember I'm the paymaster and I should be kept entirely informed of what you're doing and how you are spending my money!'

'Fuck your money! Is that all you can think about? I agreed to carry out this mission, not for money, but to try to save your people. So you do what you're best at, making pictures and leave the planning and action to us.'

'All right, Mac, I'll not question your judgement. But when you've always been top dog in a film company you find it difficult to let go of the reins to anyone else. I just hope that this man you've hooked can come up with the information you need. We've only got two days to find him and the last of my people.'

'I've told you before, Lionel, your two top stars are safe. They'll come to no harm. It's the other four that are in grave danger. So, whatever you think about it, they are my first priority.'

'Then I let you lead the way, Mac,' Durance said, leaning forward and patting Mac on the shoulder, like a scoutmaster might do to a boy scout who had won his pathfinder's badge. 'Madge, fetch that new bottle of twelve-year-old malt and the Remy Martin you bought for Mac and Sarah. I feel like a drink and I'm sure these two will join me.'

*   *   *

As soon as Mac and Sarah left the La Cucaracha Club, Arturo went to his home and collected his old diaries and address books from an old suitcase on the top shelf of his wardrobe. He found several addresses at which Moretta had lived for short periods and underlined them with a red pen. He telephoned the addresses. There was no answer from the first two and his third call was answered by a woman, who said she had only recently moved to the address and didn't know who had lived there before. Arturo had more luck with his fourth call. Moretta answered the phone. 'He just said "Hola," and waited for his caller to identify himself.

'It's me Diego, your old compadre, Arturo. I have something most important to tell you.'

There was a ten-second pause before Moretta answered. 'How did you know my telephone number, Arturo?'

'Oh, I found it in an old diary.'

'Does anyone else have this number?'

'If anyone else has this number, they didn't get it from me, Diego! I have some very important information for you. Can you come to my home?'

'Where is your home?'

'Where it has always been since we were together.'

'What is it that you want to tell me, Arturo?'

'We can't talk about it on the phone, but you could be richer by ten-thousand US dollars if you co-operate with the proposition I shall put to you.'

'Very well, I shall be with you in an hour, Arturo. I hope for your sake that this is not some sort of trick that the police have put you up to.'

'It is not a trick! Despite our present differences, I'd not betray you, Diego. I swear by the blood of Christ that I speak the truth!'

The only reply from Moretta was the sound of him replacing his receiver.

Arturo put his diaries and address book under his armchair cushion. If Moretta saw them he felt sure he'd want to destroy them. Next he took a bottle of Tequila (Moretta's favourite tipple) and two glasses from his kitchen cupboard and put them on the sofa table. I've nothing to do now for an hour, he thought, but to watch the international news.

Moretta arrived within the hour, accompanied by one of his most loyal henchmen, who Arturo recognized as Sergio Almazan, a man who enjoyed his role as Moretta's principal assassin.

After their initial exchange of greetings they both went through every room in the house.

Satisfied there was no other person in the house, they sat on the sofa opposite Arturo. Arturo fetched another glass and poured the drinks.

'So, what is the important news you have to tell me, Arturo?' Moretta said after taking a deep swig of the tequila.

Arturo related how he had met the two journalists who wanted to interview Diego Moretta and were prepared to pay him ten-thousand US dollars for the interview. He said nothing about the money that had been promised to him for locating Moretta.

All the time that Arturo was talking Moretta didn't take his eyes off him. When he had finished his account Arturo refilled their glasses.

'What were the names of these people?'

'Martin and Sabrina McFee. The man said he was always known as Marty.'

'Did they give you any proof of their identity; such as their passports or business cards?'

'No, but Marty gave me his cell phone number.'

'Where are they staying?'

'I don't know. They never told me.'

'Didn't you find that rather odd?'

Arturo's mouth began to feel dry and his heart beat faster. He took a swig of his tequila before he answered. 'Not at the time, but I see now that I should have asked them where they were staying.'

'Did you give them your address?'

'Yes, because they suggested that this would be a good place to hold the interview. It was a neutral place and the home of a trusted friend.'

'So, the final arrangement was that you were to contact me and invite me here to be interviewed. '

'Yes, Diego, that was about the size of it.'

Moretta emptied his glass and looked hard at Arturo. 'From what you have told me so far suggests to me that you have been very foolish in placing so much trust in people you didn't know and for a bottle of wine were prepared to put me at risk of capture or death. What have you to say to that?'

Arturo visibly trembled with fear. 'They seemed to be genuine and anxious to interview you. They said that your story would be highly regarded and would be published throughout the world. I was only thinking of the favourable left-wing publicity it would bring to you, apart from the fee they were prepared to pay.'

'There are many who wish to interview me, but unfortunately most of them are policemen. I believe that these two people were involved with the police in a plan to arrest me or, more likely, shoot me on sight. There is just one thing more I wish you to tell me, Arturo. Describe them to me in detail.'

Arturo drank more tequila in an attempt to clear his dried throat. 'The man looked to be in his mid-forties. He was a little under six-feet tall. He had short black hair; dark brown eyes and very white teeth. His face and hands were highly tanned and he had a nasty scar over his right eye. Although he appeared and acted like a typical Englishman, he could have been of mixed race. That's about all I can remember about him.'

'There is, I believe, just one feature you have forgotten about this man's appearance. Did he not walk with a limp?'

'Yes, Diego, I remember now that he did and he used a walking stick.'

There was a look of triumph on Moretta's face. 'Now tell me about the woman, who called herself Sábrina.'

'She was younger than her husband; possibly in the mid to late thirties. She had dark brown hair and brown eyes. She was about six inches shorter than Marty. She had a rather attractive face and figure and her skin was of a light olive colour. She too could have been of mixed race.'

Moretta nodded. 'Now I'll tell you who the fictitious Mr and Mrs Martin McFee really are. They are Eli, better known as Mac, Murphy and Sarah Murphy, British subjects who are highly ruthless adventurers. They have been hired by the Omega Film Company to recover the actors and film technicians I am holding for ransom. I have learned from various sources that this pair has been responsible for the death of several of my men and the freeing of some of my abductees. What have you to say about that, Arturo?'

'I can only say that I am truly sorry for being mistaken about these people and I beg your forgiveness,' Arturo replied in a snivelling voice.

Moretta nodded to Almazan, who walked behind Arturo's armchair, seized Arturo by the hair and yanked his head back. Then, drawing a double-edged knife from under his coat, he cut Arturo's throat from ear to ear. Arturo made a gurgling sound and sank forward dead in his chair. Almazan wiped the blade of his knife across Arturo's shirted back and replaced it under his coat.

'Leave him there, Sergio. But before we leave we must find Arturo's diaries that he said contained details of my various hideouts. Search all drawers and cupboards and every other likely hiding place.'

While Almazan was making his search, Moretta sat looking at the blood-soaked body of Arturo, drinking what remained of the tequila.

'Chief, I've spent over an hour taking this place apart and there's no sign of any diaries, or address books. What do you want me to do next?'

'If your search has been thorough then we might assume that Arturo had a good memory. Perhaps we should have used persuasive means to have tested his memory. Never mind, because fortunately, I have received information from my man in the Hotel Hilton that the Murphys are staying there in the suite next door to Lionel Durrance. No harm should come to Durrance, but the Murphys' need to be taken out of the game before they cause us any further interference. I know you are one man I can depend upon to do what is necessary, Sergio, so I'll leave the details to you.'

*   *   *

'I should have thought that we'd have had a call from Arturo by now, Mac. He can't have that many diaries and address books to look through.'

'I was beginning to think the same myself. I think I'll give him a call to gee him up a bit.'

Mac rang Arturo's number. There was no reply. He waited fifteen minutes and tried again. There was still no reply. 'He must be out; I gave him enough time to get out of the bath or off the loo.'

'I know what you're thinking, Mac, you want to pay a visit to Arturo's home and get his diaries. By doing that you'd not have to pay him anything for locating Moretta.'

'Yes, Sarah, that did cross my mind. It's now seven-thirty. About the time one would go out for a meal. If that is what he's doing, he's not likely to return much before nine-thirty, so we could go there, make a search, which shouldn't take more than a half hour, and leave before he returns.'

'What do we do if we don't find what we want?'

'We could wait outside his house until he returns and call on him a few minutes later, pretending that we'd just arrived.'

'Well, we're not doing much good at the moment, so let's see what we can find at Arturo's place, Mac. Do we need to be armed?'

'Yes, we always need to be armed in this god-forsaken country.'

They found several taxis waiting outside the hotel and Mac hired one and showed the driver Arturo's address. The journey took fifteen minutes.

As soon as the taxi was out of sight Mac and Sarah walked around the small detached house. There were no lights on in the house. Using a small hand torch Mac inspected the front and back doors and the back windows, which were screened by overhanging trees.

'This window looks as though it won't prove too difficult to prise open,' Mac said, producing a small jemmy from under his jacket. 'Take this torch and shine it at this frame, Sarah.'

It took only a minute or two for Mac to noiselessly prise open the window. He opened the window wide enough to climb over the sill and onto a kitchen worktop. He lowered himself to the floor and went over to the back door. The door was locked, but its key was in the lock. He opened the door and Sarah joined him in the kitchen.

'I don't suppose he'd keep diaries and papers in the kitchen. We'll make a start in the sitting room. Pull the curtains and I'll put the light on.'

Sarah pulled the curtains and Mac switched the light on to a scene of turmoil – cupboard and cabinet drawers pulled out and papers, books and miscellaneous items scattered on the floor. Sarah gave a startled cry as she saw the recumbent body of Arturo covered in blood on an armchair. 'He's dead, Mac, his throat has been cut. What a ghastly sight.'

'Yes, there's no doubt about that. I guess he fell foul of an earlier caller. And it's my guess it was Moretta or one of his men.'

Mac took the torch and went into the other rooms. 'They are all in the same state. They must have surely found what they were looking for. But Arturo's clothing is intact, so perhaps they thought it unlikely for him to have his books under his shirt or in his trousers pockets. But, if he has a wallet it may be in his hip pocket. I'd like to see what he has in that.' Mac pulled him out of the chair and laid him face down on the floor. As he did so the cushion fell off the chair.

'We need look no further, Mac – Arturo was sitting on his books!" Sarah said excitedly grabbing the books. She passed them to Mac who skimmed through the pages noting the addresses underlined in red and the one that had a red tick against it. 'This is the address at which he must have made contact with Moretta. Arturo would have told him of our offer and Morreta, not wanting anyone to know of his various hideouts, would come here to silence Arturo and get his diaries.'

'Yes, I'm sure that's exactly what happened,' Sarah said. 'What a stroke of luck that Arturo slipped them under his cushion before Moretta arrived.'

'Yes it was, and we must take advantage of that lucky break before Moretta skips his bolt hole.'

'What shall we do about Arturo, Mac? We can't just leave him on the carpet for his poor housekeeper to find in the morning.'

'No, you're right. Actually I was getting to like him, poor chap. He didn't deserve such a nasty end. I'll cover him with a sheet and make an anonymous call to the police. I'm sure they'll soon be around to take charge of the body.'

'I don't know about you, Mac, but I feel unclean after being in this house and before doing anything else I'd like to take a hot shower.'

'So would I. We'll go straight back to the hotel, have a

shower and a meal and then start planning how to deal with Moretta.'

*   *   *

Sergio Almazan entered the Hotel Hilton and went straight to the row of lifts and got out on the floor where Mac and Sarah's suite was located. He tapped on the door and waited a minute and then rapped on the door. Still no answer, so they must be out, he thought. He looked at his watch. A chambermaid should be making her rounds to turn down the beds in a few minutes.

The floor was deserted. Most people were in the dining rooms or in the various hotel bars. He sat down in the area opposite the lifts and picked up a newspaper from the table and held it in front of his face. A few minutes passed and he heard the lift door opening and a young uniformed maid came out onto the passageway. She tapped on a door and not receiving a reply opened the door with a master key and entered the room. A minute later she came out and went to the next room. She tapped on the door of Durrance's suite and a woman answered. She said something to the maid who went away and stopped outside the Murphys' suite. Almazan crept swiftly and quietly up behind her and seized her head in his powerful hands and violently twisted her neck until he heard it crack. Her neck was broken and she fell to the floor dead. He picked up the master key she had dropped. He then dragged her to a door of a nearby linen store. He opened the door with the key and put the dead maid under a low shelf and covered her with bales of sheets. He locked the door and returned to the Murphys' suite, opened the door and locked it behind him. He sat on a sofa which faced the door and waited for the return of his intended victims.

Almazan rarely used or carried firearms; he preferred to use daggers, stilettos or razor-sharp knives to kill his victims. He was now armed with a knife, a stiletto and a blackjack.

A half hour passed and he heard a key being inserted in the door lock. He quickly hid behind the sofa. He knew the Murphys would be armed, but guessed that they would remove their weapons before settling down to what they intended to do that evening.

'What do you want to do, Sarah, go down for dinner, or have a shower first?'

'Dinner can wait. After the day we've had I must have a shower first.'

'Okay, let's get that shower and then go down to the dining room for a decent meal,' Mac said.

They both started to take off their clothes and placed their weapons on the table in front of the sofa.

When they were completely undressed and had entered the bathroom, Almazan came out of hiding and stood listening outside the bathroom. He heard their voices through the door. They were obviously enjoying their shower. Their last one, he thought as he drew his double-edged, razor-sharp knife from its underarm sheaf.

The noise of the splashing shower and their voices

ceased. They must be drying themselves. So, they were now naked, weaponless and completely at his mercy; he would enjoy this, he thought, licking his lips as he entered the bathroom.

'What the hell do you think you're doing, bursting into a private bathroom!' Mac shouted.

'I've come to kill you,' Almazan replied, advancing towards Mac with his knife poised to strike.

Sarah threw down her towel and thrust her breasts out. 'You wouldn't waste a body like mine, would you?'

As Almazan turned to ogle Sarah's sensuous body, Mac swung into action and grabbed a deodorant spray from an overhead shelf and sprayed Almazan's gloating face. Almazan dropped his knife and screamed in agony as the fluid got into his eyes. Half-blinded, he ran back into the sitting room. Mac followed, picked up one of the pistols and struck him on the back of the head with the butt. Almazan fell to the floor unconscious.

Sarah, now in her bathrobe, came into the room holding Mac's robe. He put it on and then went through Almazan's pockets. Her removed papers from Almazan's wallet and replaced it in his hip pocket. He found a key in Almazan's jacket pocket, which he guessed would be a hotel master key that had enabled the would-be killer to get into their suite. He picked up Almazan's knife with a paper tissue and put it in its sheaf.

'What are you going to do now, ring for the police to arrest him?'

'No, if I do that the police will ask too many questions of us and might even take his side when they see the bump on his head. We haven't got time to waste being interviewed. This man came to kill us and judging by his choice of weapon I'd say he's the man who cut Arturo's throat. So, I have a better way to deal with him. Go out on the balcony, but don't turn on the light and see if there are any people sitting out on their balconies with their lights on.'

Sarah went out and saw that the rear of the building was in near darkness. 'There's nobody in view on balconies or on the area below,' she said, guessing what Mac had in mind.

Mac dragged the still unconscious Almazan onto the balcony and leant him against the balustrade. Almazan suddenly came to, cursing Mac and trying to reach for his knife. Mac bent down and grabbed his legs and raised him until he was balanced on the top of the balustrade. 'This is for Arturo!' Mac said as he tipped him over the balustrade to fall, surprisingly silently, a hundred feet to the paved area below.

Mac came back into the sitting room, locked the balcony door and drew the curtains.

'Why did you keep that key you took from his pocket?' Sarah said.

'Because, my dear, had the police found the master key on him, they would have thought it very strange that a burglar would be climbing over balustrades to rob rooms, when he had a key that opened all the rooms in the hotel.'

'Well, you certainly do think on your feet, Mac. You would have made a good secret service agent.'

'In our work you have to if you want to stay ahead of the game. But never mind all that chat. I want to get changed for dinner.'

Sarah was dressed in her usual stylish evening wear. She had put their pistols back in their hiding place at the bottom of her wardrobe and was now sitting watching television, while Mac got dressed.

'I'll be ready in a couple of ticks,' called Mac from the bedroom. 'All that activity has given me a ravenous appetite.'

Five minutes later Mac came in to the sitting room dressed in a midnight blue lounge suit of lightweight material, a light blue silk shirt and a flamboyant, dark blue, silk tie.

'My word, Mac, you look dressed to kill in that outfit,' Sarah said, with a little laugh.

'Yes, and you played a blinder in the bathroom, darling. You deserve a medal for your show-stopping performance; but you'll have to settle for the best meal on offer this evening.'

As they passed through the reception area to go to the dining room they saw several uniformed police, together with others in plain clothes, who were obviously detectives, questioning the receptionists. Hank was standing at his desk, unoccupied, but listening to what was being said. Mac went over to him. 'What's all the commotion about?' he asked.

'I thought you might know something about it, Mac,' he said with a sly grin. 'Apparently, a man, who was armed with two knives and a blackjack, has fallen from the back of the hotel and was killed. The police think he was a cat-burglar who fell off a balcony. They're trying to find out which room or suite he was burgling. But no one has come forward to report that they have been burgled. There'll be few guests in their rooms at this time, so I expect the police will be back tomorrow to question a few of the guests, to make it look like they're bothered about the death of a burglar, or whatever he was. Enjoy your meal.'

'We will, Hank.'

CHAPTER FIFTEEN

30 MARCH

Four of Diego Moretta's abducted members of Omega Films – Carol Farley, Rick Morales, Bruce Dawlish and Omar Rashid – were huddled under blankets in a dilapidated wooden building in the outermost suburbs of Bogotá. They were cold, hungry and fearful of what they might face on the morrow.

Bruce Dawlish, a cameraman, looked at his watch. 'It's 1.45 a.m. I think it's Javi's turn to do the check and he'll be around in a few minutes. They seem to take it in turn to come around every two hours.'

'Well, I hope he brings some food with him this time, I'm starving and my mouth's as dry as a badger's arse,' said Rick Morales, a young actor.

'I'm hungry, but I don't think I could face any more of that horrible food they've been giving us,' said Carol, a glamorous young starlet. 'And I'd do anything for a hot shower.'

'Never mind food! If the ransom money isn't paid by tomorrow we'll all be dead!' said Rashid, a young security man. 'What we need to be thinking about is how to break out of here before tomorrow.'

'How can we do anything?' said Dawlish, the

cameraman. 'There are three guards all armed with sub-machine guns and sidearms.'

'Well, there are four of us, if we count Carol, and they never come in armed with their AK-47s. They just have their automatic pistols holstered,' Rashid said, airing his superior knowledge of firearms. 'I have an idea of how we can overpower the guard. There's no light in here and they only use a torch when they come to check us. So, this is what we could do. Bruce, you and Rick get under your blankets and make yourselves look like three people. Pretend to be asleep and make snoring sounds. I shall stand by the door with my blanket and when Javi enters I'll throw the blanket over his head and bring him down before he can draw his pistol. As soon as I do that you two leap on top of him and pin his arms down and sit on his head so that he can't shout out. I'll then get hold of his pistol. The other two guards will probably be dozing in one of the other rooms. So, once I have his pistol we'll be in control.'

'What am I supposed to do while all this is going on?' Carol said.

'Well, you did say you'd do anything for a shower, so now's your chance to help make that possible. Strip off and stand against the wall facing the door. When the guard comes in he'll shine his torch on you. This should distract him enough for me to overpower him.'

'Well, if that's going to help us get out of this hole, here goes!' she said, pulling off her bush shirt and stepping out of her jeans.

Rashid moved quietly to the door with his blanket and waited. Dawlish and Morales humped themselves up under their blankets and started to make snoring noises.

Three minutes passed before the door opened and Javi entered. Standing by the door, he switched on his torch and shone it in the direction of where he expected his prisoners to be. They were there, snoring. As he moved his torch upwards Carol's naked body came into view. He couldn't believe his eyes as Carol opened her legs and made inviting motions. It was then that Rashid struck. He flung his blanket over the Javi's head and knocked him off his feet. Seconds later Dawlish and Morales jumped on him. Dawlish sat on his head and Morales stamped on his arms. Rashid reached under the blanket and withdrew Javi's automatic pistol from its holster, and struck him twice on the head with the barrel. Javi let out an almost inaudible cry from under the blanket and slumped into unconsciousness. Rashid removed Javi's belt, put it on and holstered the pistol. It was an Austrian made Glock 17, with a seventeen 9 mm round magazine. Enough to start a small war, he thought.

Carol, now fully clothed, flung her arms around Rashid and kissed him. 'You're my hero Omar,' she whispered. 'You should be in pictures, playing the role of an action man like Bruce Willis.'

'That's enough   no more talking!' Rashid said with new-born authority. 'All of you stay here and keep that man quiet when he comes to.'

'That'll be my pleasure,' Dawlish said. 'What are you going to do now, Omar?'

'I'm going after the other two. If I don't make it, get away from here and make a run for the nearest highway, where you should be able to bum a lift to Bogotá. Once there, go to the British Embassy.'

'Good luck,' they whispered in unison as he left the room.

Rashid, his pistol drawn, crept down the narrow passageway. He paused by the door of a room from which the sound of voices could be heard. He understood from his limited Spanish that the two men had heard a noise and one of them was going to investigate its source. 'Javi, Javi, where are you?' he called out in Spanish as he came out of the room with his pistol drawn.

Without a moment's hesitation Rashid fired three shots at the man; two at his chest and one at his head. The force of the bullets sent the man back into the room and he fell dead at the feet of the other guard. The guard grabbed his AK-47 and dived for cover behind a sofa and fired a long burst at the partially opened door. Wood chips and plaster sprayed over Rashid, but he wasn't hit. He fired two shots at the sofa. Both went through the back of the sofa, but missed the guard, who dived across the room and took cover at the side of a bureau. Rashid took a chance and exposed himself to fire several shots at the bureau. All missed the guard who returned a rapid burst of fire. One bullet struck Rashid's gun arm, causing him to drop his pistol; another bullet entered his chest.

His AK-47 magazine now empty, the guard drew his pistol. Rashid dragged himself out of sight of the guard and picked up his pistol with his left hand. As the guard came through the doorway to execute a coup de grâce, Rashid fired one shot, which lifted the top of the guard's skull. He dropped dead at Rashid's feet. Rashid coughed, gave a deep sigh and fell back dead.

'The firing's stopped and Rashid hasn't returned, so I think we'd better go now,' Dawlish said.

'Don't you think we owe it to Rashid to find out if he's still alive?' Carol said. 'The other guards haven't come here, so he must have finished them off.'

'I'll see what happened,' Morales said and left the room.

'What are you going to do with that one?' Carol said, pointing at the blanket-wrapped body.

Dawlish pulled the blanket off Javi and examined his head which was covered in blood. 'I think he's dead.' He checked his pulse. There was none. 'That blow on the head that Rashid gave him with the gun must have killed him.'

'Good riddance to the murderous bastard!' Carol cried.

Morales returned and blurted out: 'They're all dead!'

'Omar as well?' Carol asked woefully.

Morales nodded. 'I'm afraid so. He was a very brave guy. He deserves a medal for the way he saved us.'

'Well, there's nothing to keep us here now, so let's do as Omar suggested and make for a highway that'll take us back to Bogotá,' Dawlish said.

'There's no need to leave now, Bruce. Omar said for us to leave if he didn't make it and the guards were still alive. In a way, Omar did make it and all our captors are finished. So we don't need to go tramping off into the dark looking for a highway. And there's something I didn't mention – when I went to the room where the shoot-out took place, I saw a useable landline telephone. So, now all we need to do is to ring for the police and tell them what has happened and they will come and collect us and deal with the dead bodies.'

'I'm all for that, Bruce, and while we're waiting I can take a shower – if there's any hot water available,' Carol said with enthusiasm. 'Even if there isn't I'll settle for a cold one.'

'Carol, before you indulge yourself, can you see if there's any decent water, or other liquids to drink, and edible foodstuffs?' Dawlish said. 'Our guards must have been supplied with food and drink.'

'Okay, Bruce, I'll see what I can rustle up while you phone the cops,' Carol replied.

Dawlish rang the police and when he told the operator who they were, he was immediately put through to the duty officer, Captain Bejanaro, who had been instructed to contact Lieutenant Colonel Valero at any time during night or day, if any information was received about the kidnapping of the Omega Film Company's personnel.

Because of foreign pressure on the Colombian Government to take stronger action against the kidnappers, Brigadier General Perez in command of the Bogotá Police Force assigned Lieutenant Colonel Valero to be responsible for dealing with all cases involving the kidnapping of foreigners.

A few minutes later Valero was patched through to Dawlish. 'Where are you located?' was Valero's first question.

'I don't know,' Dawlish replied, 'but I'll send someone outside to see if there are any signs to indicate our location.' Turning to Morales, he said: 'Nip outside Rick and see if you can spot any road signs.'

Rick went out with a torch and was back within three minutes. 'This run-down wooden house, which is some distance from any other, seems to belong to a village called Montez.'

Dawlish relayed Rick's information to Valero.

'Ah, yes, I know the place, Mr Dawlish. The few people who do live there are mostly brigands. I shall send Captain Rodrigues and a team of officers to bring you back. He should be with you in about an hour. In the meantime don't leave the house; if you do you may be abducted again.'

'Thank you Colonel, but that's not going to happen again. We have all the firearms that our guards had and will not hesitate to use them if we have to.'

Captain Rodrigues and his men arrived within the hour, followed by two ambulances to convey the dead to the city mortuary.

'Treat that man with respect,' Carol said, pointing to the body of Rashid as he was being put into the ambulance. 'He saved our lives at the cost of his own.'

They were first taken to the police headquarters for their statements to be taken and to be photographed. After a hurried takeaway meal they were delivered to the British Embassy and seen by the duty officer, who told them to return later that day to be issued with replacement passports. He then detailed a chancery guard to take them to the Hilton Hotel.

*　　*　　*

It was late-morning and Lionel Durrance was out on the balcony eating his room-service breakfast.

Madge came out to him. 'I've been watching the news, boss. Pictures of our people were shown and Brigadier General Perez, the city's police chief, was being interviewed. The story he gave was quite different to what Bruce Dawlish told us earlier this morning. The brigadier general made it seem that his men had dealt with the kidnappers and rescued Rick Morales, Bruce Dawlish and Carol Farley. He went on to say: "Unfortunately, the other abductee, Omar Rashid, had been executed by the kidnappers before my men had arrived on the scene." That's a complete distortion of what actually happened and should be reported to the foreign secretary via our ambassador.'

'No, Madge, on no account should we contradict the police version of what happened. Let them bask in self-glory. I can't afford to upset them at this stage. I'm hoping that the good press they'll get from this incident will encourage them to make a greater effort to get the release of Harvey and Gloria. So, mum's the word for all! As soon as Rick and the others are rested they must be told not to do any interviews with the media. And when they have been issued with new passports I want them to join Harry Franklin and the others in Manaus. We'd better put Mac and Sarah in the picture and find out what they have learned from the papers they took from that dead cat-burglar, Sergio Almazan. Give them a bell and ask them to join us.'

'Did you watch the news this morning, Mac?' was the first thing Durrance said when Mac and Sarah entered his suite.

Mac and Sarah sat down before Mac answered. 'Yes we did. It was good news for a change, but sad that Omar Rashid was killed.'

'What do you think about what Brigadier General Perez had to say about the incident?'

'Well, I haven't the benefit of knowing what Bruce Dawlish and the others had to say about the rescue, but it did seem to me that Perez was milking the incident dry in an effort to gain much needed credit for the Colombian Police.'

'That's a sound assessment of his input to the interview, Mac, but I don't think it would be in our best interest to challenge his statement,' Durrance said. He went on to relate the account as given to him by Dawlish.

'With regard to Omar's actions, which saved the other three abductees but resulted in his death, is it your intention to see that his family receives some sort of award for his bravery?' Sarah asked.

'No doubt the company will provide for the needs of his wife and baby daughter, but it's not something I have the time or inclination to go into at the moment. What we must do now is focus entirely on the problem of rescuing Harvey and Gloria. In that regard, have you gained any further information about the location of Moretta, Mac?'

'No, nothing positive, Lionel, but rumours of his present whereabouts that have come to light suggest he has fled by road to Panama with members of his gang and taken his two captives with them. I shall follow up as soon as we can arrange for a flight to Panama.'

'Mac, I can't believe what I'm hearing! How does this man, his gang and their two captives, cross the border of another country without falling foul of that country's immigration authorities! Furthermore, where could they stay undiscovered in Panama, when the abduction of my people is international news?'

'Lionel, you're forgetting what power and influence this man Moretta exercises. He and his men will know every back door to any of Colombia's neighbouring countries. He also has many contacts with members of the drug cartels, gun-runners and the left-wing insurgents who have little or no respect for border controls. He and his gang will be sheltered and protected by those groups, who may believe that by doing so they will be able to receive a share of the twenty-million pounds sterling that Moretta hopes to get when he delivers your two stars.'

'All right, Mac, I bow to your superior knowledge of such dark people. But the deadline for the payment of the ransom is tomorrow! So, what are you planning to do?'

'I haven't decided yet, but be assured I shall not waste another minute in deciding my course of action. With regard to Moretta's threats about what he'll do if he doesn't get paid by tomorrow, you can forget them. If he isn't paid by you, he'll probably sell them to the highest bidder. This is a common practice with these kidnappers. Now, if you'll excuse us, Sarah and I have much to do.'

'I'll leave it to you, Mac. Don't let me down.'

Mac ignored his remark as he and Sarah walked out of the room, followed by Madge, who hugged them both and whispered, 'Good luck to you both and don't take needless risks.'

'Thanks, Madge. We'll do our best to stay alive, but remember my regimental motto: He who dares wins!'

Back in their suite Mac and Sarah went through all of the documents and papers.

'Well, there's nothing here that points to where Moretta is likely to be hiding in Panama,' Mac said.

'On another matter, Mac, you mentioned to Lionel that you were booking a flight to Panama. We can't go there without our weapons and we can't take them out by air.'

'You're right, Sarah, I'm afraid I wasn't thinking straight. I'll ask Hank if he has any ideas as to how we can smuggle our weapons into Panama.'

Mac and Sarah went down to the reception. Hank, who had just come on duty, was standing at his desk. Mac caught his eye and he beckoned them over.

'If it is private business you wish to discuss we'd better go into my office.'

'It certainly is, Hank,' said Mac as he and Sarah followed him into the office. 'We've heard rumours that Moretta has crossed into Panama with his two high-valued remaining abductees. We're going after him, but we can't go by air carrying weapons.'

'So you want to know how to sneak in by road, eh?'

'Yes, that's about the size of it!'

'Well, you're in luck, because I have been advised by our Panama office that your man is in cahoots with a gang of drug smugglers who are attempting to ship a large amount of cocaine into the States. It is thought that tomorrow evening they will attempt to go by sea in a very large go-fast boat, with a huge cargo of cocaine, which could have a street value of over $2,000,000. They will speed up the California coastline, at 50 to 80 knots, avoiding our coastguard patrols by staying outside the territorial limits until they find an unguarded spot on the coast to land their cargo.'

'Go-fast boats   they're a new one on me, Hank.'

'They've been around since the Prohibition era. They were called "rum-runners" when they were used to transfer rum from larger vessels waiting outside the territorial waters. More recently they were called "cigarette boats" when they were used to smuggle cigarettes from Canada to the US.'

'Well, Hank, it wouldn't surprise me if they were now to be used by Moretta to smuggle film stars into the States, where he might make a deal with one of the major film studios for a ransom pay-off for them.'

'You could be right about that, Mac. But now to business; I'm leaving this afternoon to take charge of our Panama section, so you're welcome to come with me and Carlos, who'll be driving. Wait in reception, where Carlos will pick us up at 14.00 hours. I'll need to go to my apartment, to get, as you Brits might say, "tooled up" before we leave.'

'How far is it from Bogotá to Panama City, Hank?'

'It's nearly 500 miles and over rough country. But the way Carlos drives should get us there in eight or nine hours. You should get a good lunch and then relax until we're ready to go.'

'Right, we'll do just that. See you later, Hank.'

As they came out of Hank's office a hotel porter scurried away from Hank's desk. 'That looked to me as though that man had been listening outside,' Sarah remarked.

'Never mind that now. He was probably just a nosy little man with nothing better to do. Let's get an early lunch. Afterwards, we'll do like Hank and get tooled up!'

After a hurried lunch, Mac and Sarah returned to their suite and mustered their weapons: two automatic pistols fitted with sound moderators, and Mac's swordstick.

'I've been looking at a map of the route we'll be taking and we'll be passing some very high ground, so we'd better put on our heaviest coats, Sarah.'

Mac and Sarah sat waiting in reception and at exactly 2 p.m. Carlos walked into the reception and Hank left his office.

'Okay, folks, you're now going to get the drive of your life. My place first, Carlos.'

They climbed in, Hank alongside Carlos and Mac and Sarah in the back. Ten minutes later they arrived at Hank's apartment in a high-rise block in the city centre.

'Come up with me and we'll have one for the road while I get my gear together.'

Hank led them into his sitting room. That's odd, he thought, I'm sure I locked the door before I left this morning. 'Help yourselves to a drink,' he said, pointing to a bottle of brandy standing on a small bar in the corner of the room. He then went in to his bedroom, returning a minute later with a leather suitcase. Carlos poured the drinks for the others, but not for himself.

The heavy drapes at the tall windows suddenly parted and a man emerged. He held an automatic pistol fitted with a sound moderator. He pointed the pistol at each member of the group in turn, and then shifted his aim to remain on Hank. 'Señor Henri de Poitier, I have been ordered to kill you.' Hank leapt at the man as he fired. The bullet hit Hank in his chest and he collided with the man as he fell to the floor. The man fired again and the bullet went into the wall. He aimed at Hank again, but Mac strode forward and struck his hand a vicious blow with his swordstick. The man screamed with pain and dropped the pistol and before he could retrieve it with his other hand Mac activated his swordstick and drove its blade into the man's chest. The man still tried to retrieve his weapon until Sarah drew her pistol and shot him in the head.

Saran knelt down beside Hank and checked his wound. 'The bullet's missed all your vital organs, Hank, but you need urgent medical attention.'

'I know, so please listen carefully to what I have to say – Mac, you and Sarah must go on without me. Carlos is to contact our people in Panama and tell them what happened and that Carl Miller is to take charge of the operation and is to co-operate with Mac and Sarah Murphy. They are in pursuit of Diego Moretta, who holds two movie stars for ransom. Next, Carlos, get in touch with my local agents and tell them I need the urgent attention of our tame surgeon and to have my apartment cleaned up. Mac, take this case with you. There's some very useful high explosives in it. Sarah, please fetch some pillows from my bedroom and a bottle of water. I don't expect to be on my own for long but I want to be comfortable.'

'We could get you on your bed, Hank,' Mac said.

'I know, but someone might come to check if their killer has been successful. If I'm here I can get the first shot off as he comes through that door. There's a pistol in that case – leave it with me, Mac.'

Mac took out the pistol, checked that it was loaded and placed it beside Hank.

'Have you made those calls, Carlos?'

'Yes, Chief, and everyone who needs to know has your instructions.'

'Well, get off then,' Hank said with a croak.

They made their farewells and went down to the car.

When they had passed the outskirts of the city the volume of traffic lessened and Carlos maintained an 80 mph speed for most of the journey. Sarah slept for most of the time and Mac did a spell of driving to give Carlos a break.

When Carlos had been driving for about three hours he stopped the car, took a jerrican from the boot and topped up the vehicle's tank. Next he produced a picnic hamper containing a variety of sandwiches, soft drinks and two large thermos flasks – coffee in one and tea for the British in the other. They took a 20-minute break and continued the journey.

They arrived at their destination shortly before midnight. Carlos pulled up outside a large detached house on a poorly lit dirt road, not far from the coast.

Mac noted there were few other buildings in sight. 'I thought we were going to Panama City, Carlos?' Mac said as they got out of the car.

'No, the CIA office is in Panama City, but this is near where the action is going to take place,' Carlos replied.

Carlos led them up the steps to the house, which from the outside appeared to be in total darkness. He rang a doorbell and the door was opened within seconds by a tall, thickset, ruddy-faced man with long, greying black hair. 'Welcome folks, come in. I'm Carl Miller. I know you, Carlos, and I guess you two must be Mac and Sarah Murphy. I know we haven't met before, but I've heard plenty of good things about you, from Hank.'

They followed Miller into a large sitting room, where

five tough looking men were grouped around a coffee table playing craps.

'Okay, guys. put your toys away – we've got company. Mac and Sarah are here to join the action. They've had a long, hard drive getting here so I want to give them a very quick briefing about what we intend to carry out tomorrow evening, so they can get their heads down.' He then introduced the five men: 'Chuck Harden, Danny Krantz, Jake Feltz, Earl Harper and Butch Lardner. Now, off you lot to get your heads down and lay off the booze. If we're successful tomorrow I'll throw a party for you!'

The five agents said their goodnights and trooped off to their bedrooms.

'I'm sure you'd like to hear the news about Hank. Our medic in Bogotá was on the scene in minutes and he treated Hank and got him into our private clinic to recover. We also heard that you saved his life and rid the world of another scumbag.'

'So, what's the plot for tomorrow, Carl?'

'Well, we have it on good authority that the cocaine cowboys intend to leave Panama's territorial waters on a large go-fast boat and head north as far as Frisco to off-load about two thousand Ks of coke.'

'Yes, Hank told me all about that, but what's Diego Moretta's connection?'

'That sonofabitch is in tight with the drug cartels and they have promised him a lift to the States with a couple of kidnapped film stars. If they get them there they'll expect a big cut of the ransom money.'

'How do you propose to catch them, Carl, when they're heading north at such high speed?'

'Because we too have a large go-fast boat and we'll engage them where they are anchored and if they don't surrender we'll blow them out of the water!'

'Hey, just a minute, Carl, what about their two abducted passengers?' Sarah said.

'Oh, don't take me too literally, Sarah, I'm sure we can take them without sinking the boat.'

'What armament are you toting, Carl?'

'We have a .50 calibre machine gun, RPGs, M18 Armalite rifles and Smith and Wesson 1006 pistols.'

'Bloody hell, Carl, that's some arsenal you're carrying. What about the opposition; what'll we be facing from them?'

'They'll most likely be armed with AK-47 assault rifles, sundry handguns and hand grenades.'

'If this briefing is going on much longer I'll make some coffee,' Sarah interposed.

'Great the kitchen's through there, Sarah,' Carl said, pointing at a door.

'Would it be possible for you, Carl, to close with them and give me covering fire if I could board their boat?

'Yeah, but you'd have to be damned quick about it and I know you've got a gammy left leg.'

'What I suggest is that you rake their deck with your .50 calibre and do a slow pass at their stern to allow me to get aboard and take cover. I'll take Hank's case of explosives with me and when I've freed Harvey and

Gloria I'll leave it where it'll do most good. We'll then jump overboard, to be picked up by you while you're giving us covering fire and firing at the case.'

'Boy-oh-boy, Mac, you make it all sound like a walk in a ball park!'

'Well, you've got to dare if you want to win, Carl!'

'What's Sarah going to be doing while this is all going on?'

'If you've got a sniper's rifle aboard, I might be the one to make sure that case of explosives does the job,' Sarah said as she brought the coffee cups in.

Mac nodded. 'Yes, my darling wife is damn near as good as Annie Oakley with a sniper's rifle.'

'Then welcome aboard, Sarah,' Carl said with a wide grin.

CHAPTER SIXTEEN

31 MARCH

It was high noon and Mac, Sarah and the CIA agents were checking their weapons and loading them aboard their go-fast boat.

'Listen up, men,' said Carl, 'I've been watching through my binoculars at the coke smugglers ferrying their cargo, by motorboat, out to their boat all morning. I figure they've just about got it all loaded and will probably set off late afternoon, so that they will be passing the California coast during the night. They'll not be showing their navigation or any other lights to draw attention to their passage.'

'What do you aim to do, Carl?' Mac asked. 'Intercept them mid-afternoon, when the sun will be on their port side?'

'Yes, that's the ticket, Mac. Now, we've done what we have to do, this is the order of battle for 15.00 hours: I'll be taking the wheel with Chuck as back-up if I get hit. Butch, you and Jake man the machine gun and when we're making our approach, open up and rake the foredeck and bridge to stop them speeding away. But whatever you do don't cause any damage that will sink the boat or hit anyone below deck. As soon as we make our slowed down pass of their stern, Mac is going to get onto the stern deck with the case of bangers. Nobody fire near that case until Mac and the two abductees are clear of the boat. Earl and Danny, you make sure you're ready to help Mac and the other two get aboard. Are there any questions?'

'Yes, Chief, where's the sniper's rifle I'm to use?' Sarah said.

Earl collected the rifle from a rack on the boat and handed it to Sarah. She checked the action and then practised sighting it at rocks and other objects around the inlet where their go-fast boat was anchored.

At 14.45 hours, Carl ordered everyone to board the boat and to take up their positions. He took control and the boat shot forward in the direction of where the drug smugglers' boat was anchored. As soon as they were in range of the other vessel Butch and Jake let loose with their machine gun, firing at the bridge and the foredeck. Two of the crew were hit as they tried to wind up the anchor and the helmsman was shot at the wheel.

'Get ready to board her, Mac we're going to make a pass at their stern ten seconds from now.'

As soon as their boat passed the stern of the drug-smugglers' boat, Mac picked up the case and hurled it onto the stern as he leapt and caught the stern's rail. He pulled himself onto the deck and took cover behind a raised hatch cover.

Butch and Jake continued to fire at any of the enemy crew who tried to fire on Mac's position.

Below decks, Harvey and Gloria were in a cabin, being held at gunpoint by two of Moretta's men.

'Boss, we're done for if we don't surrender,' said one of the men.

Moretta ignored him, but ripped the shirt off the man's back and tied it to a rifle barrel. He then eased the cabin's glass roof window open and waved his surrender flag up through it. 'Fire another shot at this boat, or try to stop us and my two prisoners will die!' he shouted.

'Cease fire!' Carl ordered.

Moretta's two men turned away from their charges to see what Moretta would do next.

Harvey picked up a glass fruit bowl and smashed it down on the head of the man nearest to him. The man dropped his pistol. Harvey quickly scooped it up from the floor and shot the other man in the arm. The man dropped his weapon and fell forward in front of Harvey. Moretta spun round and fired two shots at Harvey. Both shots hit the wounded man in the back. One of the bullets passed through his body and hit Harvey in his left shoulder. Believing that Harvey, who was feigning death under the dead gunman's body, was also dead, Moretta grabbed Gloria's arm and dragged her out of the cabin and onto the deck. Holding her arm, he put his pistol to the side of her head. 'Let us move off now or this woman dies!' he shouted. Still holding Gloria's arm, he turned to look up to the bridge where two crewmen stood ready. He gave them a triumphant wave with his other hand, which held his pistol. It was then that his head exploded as a bullet entered his skull.

'That was a damn fine shot you made, Sarah,' Carl said.

'Yes, I hope I can do as well aiming at that case of explosives,' Sarah replied.

'Butch, you cover that bridge, to make sure they don't take off!'

Mac went down to the cabin to find that Harvey had managed to disentangle himself from the dead gunman. 'Where are you hit, kid?'

'In my left shoulder.'

Mac put a lifebelt on him and told Gloria to put one on.

'I'm okay, pal, I've got medals for swimming. Let's put Harvey over the side and I'll jump in with you and wait to be picked up.'

They gently lowered Harvey over the side and both jumped in.

'The water is lovely and refreshing for someone who hasn't had a shower for two weeks,' Gloria said with a girlish giggle. 'Let's swim towards your boat, pulling Harvey along.'

They had swum about 50 yards towards the boat when there was a tremendous explosion in their rear. They turned to see the debris of the go-fast boat raining down and the remains of the boat sinking with its billion-dollar cargo of cocaine.

EPILOGUE

Hugo Bickerstaff was briefing Sir Roland Plenderleith, the British Ambassador in Bogotá about the rescue of the last two abducted film actors. 'I'm sure you will be pleased to hear, Your Excellency, that Harvey Rheingold and Gloria Duprez were rescued by Mac and Sarah Murphy. Harvey was wounded in the left shoulder during the rescue and is now recovering in the city hospital. The Murphys are now on their way home to the UK.'

The ambassador beamed with pleasure. 'Yes, that certainly is good news, Hugo. It will at least stop the seemingly endless exchange of diplomatic notes between London and Bogotá, which have caused us so much extra work. I shall be sending my report to the Foreign and Commonwealth Office, so please let me have a detailed report of all you've been able to gather about the whole affair. Try not to disparage the efforts of the police and the military for their lack of a determined effort to rescue the abductees. For, if you do so, Hugh, it will only engender ill-feeling in diplomatic circles.'

'Yes, Your Excellency, I shall bear your comments in mind and make the report my next job of the day.'

*   *   *

Sir Randolph Blandish and Rupert Bartram, the Director of the Secret Intelligence Service (better known as MI6) were closeted in Sir Randolph's office to discuss the outcome of the mission to rescue the abducted Omega Film Company's employees.

'I presume you have seen the report from our ambassador in Bogotá, Rupert?'

'Yes, sir, I have received it and the many others that have been received.'

'What are your views as to their veracity about how the mission was conducted?'

'I have to be frank, sir; from what I have heard from unlikely, but friendly sources, the reports have been deliberately watered down and undeserved credit has been given to the action taken by the police and the military to avoid rocking the boat in diplomatic circles.'

'So, where should the credit go?'

'To Mac and Sarah Murphy, sir. They set about the task with resolute will and were ruthless in their dealings with the uncompromising bandits who held the abductees.'

'So, I took the right decision when I authorized the Murphys to undertake the mission?'

'Yes, sir, but they were not afforded very much support by HM's Government.'

'Well, I'm sure you realize we have every right to expect that British citizens will be protected when they visit foreign countries and the only action we can take is to send strong diplomatic notes to the governments of the countries where the kidnapped British subjects are held. And, unlike other countries, we have resolved never to pay ransoms to secure their freedom. To pay ransoms would only make British subjects more vulnerable when visiting countries, where abduction for ransom is a common practice.'

'With due respect, sir, I am aware of the present government policy with regard to the abduction of British subjects abroad. What I would like to know is whether it is your intention to cite the Murphys for an award for their gallantry; if not that, perhaps something like a CBE, or at least an OBE?'

Sir Randolph looked thoughtful. 'I have to say, I haven't really given the matter much thought. But I don't think it would be in our best interests to show we agreed entirely with the way they carry out their missions. Eli Murphy does often merit the description of being a loose cannon! But to appease public opinion, I suppose we could put him up for an MBE in the New Year's Honours List.'

'Sir, I have to say that such an award would be an insult to them. And, as for so-called loose cannons, they sometimes get the job done when those chained to bureaucracy and political correctness often fail. I admit I have a sneaking regard for the Murphys and would welcome them to join our Secret Intelligence Service.'

Sir Randolph's eyebrows almost reached his hairline. 'You're completely out of order, Rupert, and if you want to retain your position, never again voice such an opinion!'

'Very well, sir; is that all?'

'Yes, Rupert   that is all!'

*　　*　　*

Oscar Durkin, the Deputy Director of the CIA, was visiting Henri de Poitier in the clinic, where he was recovering from his wound. 'Your doctor tells me you'll be fit to return to duty in a couple of days, Hank. Of course you won't be remaining in Colombia. Your cover as VIP concierge has been blown wide open. So, when you're discharged from here you should report back to Langley for re-assignment. From what you say about the help you got from those gung-ho Murphys, the view of our top people is that they are deserving of a high award.'

'I couldn't agree more, sir,' Hank replied. 'They deserve the highest award The Medal of Honour, but that may only be awarded to United States citizens.'

*　　*　　*

Lionel Durrance and Madge Burton had joined Harry Franklin and the cast and technicians to work on the film *Crisis in Colombia* in Manaus, Brazil.

'Well, Harry, things are certainly looking good for the future. Harvey's almost fit enough to join the film lot and with all the favourable media coverage we've been getting our film should be a block-busting hit!'

'Yes, Lionel, and it'll all be due to what the Murphys did in rescuing our people. I take back what I said about Harvey not being able to portray an action man. He seems to have grown a couple of inches and gained the respect of the entire cast and crew.'

'That's splendid! We'll make a fresh start tomorrow, Harry, so see that everyone gets an early night and is up early, all bright and bushy-tailed in the morning.'

* * *

About nine months after Mac and Sarah returned to their home in Cambridge with a £1,000,000 payoff from Omega Films, they were having breakfast, discussing their plans for the weekend, when the letter flap banged and there was a plopping sound as the mail dropped on the hall carpet.

'I'll get it, Mac,' Sarah said rising from her chair.

'From the sound it made coming through the door it's probably mostly junk mail,' Mac said as he spread marmalade on a slice of toast.

Sarah returned a minute later with two letters. 'I've binned all the junk mail,' she said with a laugh. 'I bet you can't guess what I've got here,' she said, waving an opened envelope.'

'No, I'm not in a guessing mood   surprise me!'

'I have here two tickets for the premiere showing of *Crisis in Colombia* at the Odeon, Leicester Square, on Saturday.'

They said nothing, but exchanged meaningful glances.

The End

ND - #0482 - 270225 - C0 - 203/127/19 - PB - 9781861510853 - Matt Lamination